TOM SWIFT

young inventor

Don't Miss Tom's Other Adventures!

TOM SWIFT
young inventor

#6 UNDER THE RADAR

By Victor Appleton

Aladdin Paperbacks
New York London Toronto Sydney

❧

ALADDIN PAPERBACKS
An imprint of Simon & Schuster Children's Publishing Division
1230 Avenue of the Americas, New York, NY 10020
Copyright © 2007 by Simon & Schuster, Inc.

Designed by Lisa Vega
The text of this book was set in Weiss.
Manufactured in the United States of America
First Aladdin Paperbacks edition October 2007
2 4 6 8 10 9 7 5 3 1

Library of Congress Control Number 2007922547
ISBN-13: 978-1-4169-3644-2

Contents

UNDER THE RADAR

Kidnapped!

Summertime is the best.

It's better than best, actually. In my book, summer is an entire order of magnitude greater than best.

Hey, I love every season, and yeah, we get all four of them here in Shopton. But how can summer *not* be the favorite? No school, no homework, extra sleep, tons of quality time in my personal lab. And did I mention the extra sleep? Dude, I'm sixteen. If I could, I'd sleep more than Emma, my sister's lazy cat.

But here's the best thing about summer: Dad's company always downshifts in July and August, with employees going off on vacations and whatnot. That means Dad has more time to chill with me.

Example: The first Saturday in July, Dad and I were hiking in Theodore Roosevelt State Park, just

east of town. For such a techno-genius, Dad always seemed most relaxed outdoors in natural settings— the wilder the better. Casmir Trent, Dad's body- guard, was with us too; Casmir's a great guy, like an uncle to me. A former international kickboxing champion with a physique chiseled like a diamond, Casmir is the man you want watching your back. As we passed through the incredible rainbow mist at the base of Shopton Falls, I suddenly jogged around a bend, ahead of my companions. Then I pushed the button on a controller I held in my palm . . . and stood stock-still.

Seconds later Dad and Casmir rounded the bend.

"Okay, Tom, *now* where are you?" called Casmir, rubbing the top of his angular, shaved head.

I stood no more than twenty feet directly in front of them. I didn't answer. I didn't move.

"Come on, Ghost Recon," said Dad, looking around. "I already told you I'm impressed."

I hopped side to side a few times.

"See me now?" I asked.

Dad and Casmir both turned toward the sound of my voice.

"Amazing," said Casmir with a grin. "No, I don't."

Dad was looking right at me, so I started waving my arms.

"Ah," he said. "Now I'm seeing something . . . just a subtle blur in the vision field. Tom, that's fantastic."

I grinned proudly. You see, I was showing off my latest invention to my teacher.

Most folks know my dad as Thomas Swift, founder and owner of Swift Enterprises, the world-renowned company dedicated to better living through high technology. To me, of course, he's Dad. But the fact is, he's *more* than a dad to me—he's my mentor, the guy who taught me almost everything I know about science, technology, and using my imagination.

So whenever I put together something new in my lab, I want to show it to him. I want his stamp of approval.

That day, I was testing the prototype of my new Chameleon Suit. It's a full-body camouflage array plus a mask, all made of a special "intelligent" fabric that can change colors in response to local stimuli.

"So what's your material?" asked my dad. "Nanoplastic?"

"Close," I said. I deactivated the suit and peeled off the mask as Dad and Casmir approached. "It's actually nanofabric, but it works on the same principle as the Speedster. Instead of shape-memory polymers, I used silicon nanospheres coated in microphotoreceptors."

"Could you put it in layman's terms?" asked Casmir with a wry grin.

I laughed. "Sorry," I said. I held out the mask for Casmir to examine the fabric. "The surface isn't a continuous piece of material. You can't see it—not without a microscope, anyway—but it's actually composed of millions of tiny, magnetically linked spheres."

"You're making fun of me, right?" said Casmir.

"No, no," I said. "This is for real, man. And each nanosphere is coated with dozens of cell-size, light-sensitive photoreceptors, all linked in a network. This network can detect and code surrounding color patterns and then quickly mimic them."

Dad nodded happily, running his hand over the rough, scratchy surface of the fabric. "Casmir, this stuff is similar to the morphing nanoplastic in our Swift Speedster, the SW-1," he said. "That car uses smart, active materials that magnetically reconfigure themselves on a microscopic level for shape-shifting."

"But in my Chameleon Suit," I said, "the materials don't change shape. Instead, they change color—but they do it very fast, in the blink of an eye."

"This all sounds suspiciously like magic," said Casmir, raising his bushy eyebrows.

"Well, you've heard the old Arthur C. Clarke quote, of course," said my dad, eyes twinkling.

"No sir, but I get the feeling I will now," said Casmir.

Dad laughed and gestured to me.

"It's my favorite quote of all time, Casmir," I said. Then I cleared my throat and deepened my voice dramatically. "Mr. Clarke said, 'Any sufficiently advanced technology is indistinguishable from magic.'"

Casmir Trent nodded. "I like that," he said.

"Me too," I said.

We started hiking again. The park trails were wide, so we walked side by side. Theodore Roosevelt State Park is one of my favorite places in the world. Tucked between Mount Shopton to the north and a jagged ridge called Blue Crest to the south, the valley is full of wildlife and tall, old pines. The place just totally and seriously rocks.

"Anyway," said my dad, "I imagine a garment that

lets you blend into your surroundings will be a very popular item. We could sell a *lot* of these. Have you tested it in other types of environments?"

"A few," I said. "It works well in trees or bushes, as you just saw, and against any monochromatic background—an adobe wall, a rock cliff, any snowscape, places like that. And it's awesome in dark areas or deep shadows; you totally vanish. But it doesn't do as well in a really dynamic environment, like a crowded street or a mall or something."

"Yes, that makes sense," said Dad.

We were still a good mile from the trailhead where we'd parked our Land Rover. A path fork was just ahead. One fork led back down to the trailhead; the other ran north up Mount Shopton in a series of switchbacks. As I glanced at the trail marker, a white wooden post, I heard the rumble of an engine.

Casmir frowned. "This area is off-limits to vehicles," he said, stepping instinctively in front of us.

"Maybe it's a ranger patrol," I said. "They drive up here sometimes for trail maintenance."

"You've seen this?" asked Casmir sharply.

Casmir's job is to be suspicious, so I didn't take his tone personally. "Yeah," I said.

Casmir visibly relaxed. He turned to me with a smile and started to speak.

And of course, that's when it happened.

A big black Jeep Liberty suddenly roared around the trail's curve, kicking up a cloud of dust and gravel. Casmir barely had time to spin around when the Jeep veered into him, clipping him with its front fender and knocking him a good ten feet through the air. I didn't see Casmir land because the Jeep swerved into a crazy power-slide between us. While still moving, its doors burst open.

Four guys in ski masks leaped out.

"Run, Tom!" shouted Dad.

I didn't need a second warning; I took off like a shot. My camo suit was floppy and heavy and difficult to run in, so I figured I was toast. But all four of the masked men went straight for Dad. When I glanced back, they were hauling him into the Jeep.

I skidded to a halt.

"Don't stop, Tom!" cried my dad. "Run! Run!"

It was one of the worst moments of my life. I knew I couldn't save Dad. But I couldn't just . . . flee. Almost without thinking, I punched the controller button in my hand. The Chameleon Suit activated.

I could hear strips of duct tape being torn off a roll as the kidnappers secured my father in the back of the Jeep. Then two of the masked men leaped out.

"He was right there!" growled one.

"He disappeared!" cried the other.

Then the driver's window rolled down. Another masked face leaned out.

"Forget sonny boy!" snarled the voice—of a woman! "Ya'll get back in the car. Let's get gone!"

I was shaking with adrenaline, fear, and anger, as you might imagine. But among all the other things he taught me, Dad always stressed how important it is to observe things carefully, *especially* when you're excited.

Learn the art of observation, Tom, he always said. *Make it a habit.*

So I remained just rational enough to note the woman's strong Southern drawl. And I noted that the Jeep took the upper trail toward the Mount Sharpton switchbacks, not the one heading downhill toward the trailhead.

Then I ran to Casmir Trent.

He was unconscious, crumpled in a heap, and his left leg looked broken or dislocated. His face was scraped and bleeding, too. It looked bad.

Quickly I pulled up my sleeve to reveal my wristwatch.

"We've got a serious emergency, Q.U.I.P.," I said. "This is code red."

The wristwatch beeped once, and then a grim voice barked, "I've got 9-1-1 on the line."

"Thanks," I said.

My "wristwatch," of course, is way more than just a timepiece. It's a full wireless communications center and, usually, the place where Q.U.I.P. resides. Q.U.I.P. (a.k.a. Quantum Utilizing Interactive Processor) is a chip; it's also my man Friday, an intelligent PDA that I consider my backup brain.

The 9-1-1 dispatcher came on, and I gave her a frenzied summary of what just happened. Then with Q.U.I.P.'s help I relayed the coordinates for our location.

"We'll have a medivac over you in five minutes," she said coolly.

"What about my dad?" I said. I could still hear the Jeep roaring back and forth up the switchback trail above me.

"We have a police chopper heading for Mount Shopton," she replied. "Now I'm going to talk to you

9

about the victim there for the next few minutes."

"Right," I said. "Of course."

I kneeled next to Casmir, answering her questions and following her first-aid instructions. Minutes later I heard the thrumming of a helicopter. I could also hear sirens in the distance, coming from the direction of the park's main road.

Then, abruptly, a massive explosion rattled the branches all around me. As the concussive wave passed, I jumped to my feet and stared up the mountainside.

Halfway up the slope of Mount Shopton, a huge fireball rose into the air!

2

Special Agent

The next morning, I sat in the executive conference room on the thirtieth floor of Swift Tower, headquarters of Dad's company. To my right sat my mother, looking calm but a little dazed. My sister, Sandy, sat fidgeting to my right. Around the long oval table, key members of Dad's staff silently perused copies of the Shopton Police report.

A tall woman burst into the room.

"Sorry I'm late," she said, briskly sitting on the far side of my mother.

Dad once called Yvonne Williams, his vice president and chief financial officer at Swift Enterprises, "the most competent person I've ever met." She isn't a scientist or engineer, but her head for business is scary good. Because of her capable oversight of

company finances, Dad had always had more time to focus on his research projects.

She placed a hand on Mom's arm. "I'm so sorry, Mary. This is terrible. But you hang in there. We'll get to the bottom of this."

"Thanks, Yvonne," replied my mom quietly.

Yvonne and her husband, Leonard Williams, a patent attorney, were also good family friends. Leonard was a great football player in college; he still held the Colonial Conference season record for quarterback sacks. Dad and I loved talking football with him.

Yvonne looked around the room. "As you all know, this is more than a company crisis," she said. "It's a personal one. And I, for one, am not willing to rely on the Shopton Police to handle it alone."

"Hear, hear!" called Harlan Ames, head of security. He sat directly across the table from me.

"The reason I'm late is that the district attorney is talking to federal authorities now, which is good news, I hope," said Yvonne. "As a result, however, the FBI plans to issue dozens of fairly *intrusive* requests for background info on Swift operations. I had to attend to that."

Hector Rodriguez, Dad's personal assistant, shook

his head in disgust. "I fielded about eight million phone calls this morning from investigators asking foolish personal questions," he said. Hector was my dad's right-hand man, and he was taking the kidnapping news pretty hard. "Why aren't they out investigating Mr. Swift's *enemies* instead of *us*?"

"Dad doesn't have enemies," I said.

"Rivals, then," said Hector. I knew who he was talking about: Foger Utility Group. FUG was never one to shy from playing dirty. But I figured even Randall Foger wouldn't stoop to kidnapping a competitor.

"What about TRB?" blurted my sister.

I started to answer and then had to nod. "Good point," I conceded.

The Road Back, or TRB, was a fringe radical group opposed to all forms of modern science and technology. As a result of this belief, they saw high-tech companies like Swift Enterprises and Foger Utility Group as evil.

"Exactly!" exclaimed Hector. "Instead of snooping through Mr. Swift's PDA, they should be tracking down those insane fanatics."

"I'm sure they're checking out all the obvious suspects, Hector," said my mom gently. She really valued Hector's loyalty to her husband. "The police are just being thorough."

Harlan Ames nodded at this. "You never know where you might find a connection that turns out to be a clue," he said.

Hector sighed. "I suppose so."

Yvonne Williams nodded at Mr. Ames. "What do you have for us, Harlan?"

Harlan held up the local police's report. "According to this, the Jeep was totally destroyed in that fireball," he said. Harlan *looks* like a congenial, gray-haired grandfather, but he's gruff and tough as nails. He was an FBI field agent for twenty years before Dad hired him as head of security for Swift Enterprises. "The good news: Nobody was in the vehicle when it exploded. The bad news: They found absolutely no trace of an escape from the site. Nothing!"

"And no word from the kidnappers?" asked Yvonne. "No ransom demand?"

Harlan shook his head grimly. "Nothing yet," he said. "We're taping every incoming call, and the Geo-Net Tracer software is running. It should be a good test."

Swift's computer-lab folks were developing an amazing new system that could instantly trace and map the geographical origin of cell phone calls.

Yvonne looked at my mom. "What about your home phones, Mary?" she asked.

"Monitored," said Mom. She held up a cell phone. "All calls from unrecognized numbers will forward automatically to my cell." I could see her hand shaking a bit, so I wrapped my arm around her shoulder.

"He'll be okay, Mom," I said.

She gave me a thin smile. "I know." Then she said, "What's the latest on Casmir?"

"I've got Q.U.I.P. monitoring the hospital updates," I said. I held up my wrist unit. "Q.U.I.P.?"

"Yes, my liege," he replied in an English accent.

I rolled my eyes. "You'd better have good news on Casmir Trent."

"Oh yes," said Q.U.I.P. "Mr. Trent is stabilized, conscious, doing quite well, actually. Multiple rib fractures, a broken collarbone, some contusions, and so forth. The concussion was second degree, but motor skills are fine, no memory deficits, no disorientation."

"Prognosis?" I asked.

"Looks good, man!"

I squinted at my wrist. "Q.U.I.P., you're programmed to be a data-rich artificial intelligence. Can we get some detail?"

Q.U.I.P. sighed. "I'm monitoring the hospital's online report from the care station. Under 'prognosis,' it reads, 'Looks good.'"

"Oh," I said.

To my left, Sandy, squirmed. She's fifteen, just a year younger than me. Sandy's too smart for her own good, so she gets bored easily. In this case she was anxious to get out and start looking for Dad. She's a big fan of math puzzles, brainteasers, and mysteries. I knew how Sandy thought: She was figuring she could crack the case on her own if she could just get out and gather a few clues.

To be perfectly honest, I felt likewise.

"So have we done all we can?" asked Yvonne.

Harlan Ames stood up. "I'm taking our security team up to the kidnapping site this morning," he said. He turned to my mother with a grim, earnest look. "I assure you that this company will use all available resources to find Mr. Swift."

Suddenly the conference room door burst open. Mrs. Henderson, Yvonne Williams's personal assistant, stood in the doorway.

"I'm sorry, Ms. Williams," she said. "These folks insisted on seeing you . . . immediately."

She stepped aside as three men in dark suits filed in, followed by a very neat and severe-looking woman in a dark blue jacket and skirt. Behind them, two Swift security guards slipped in as well. Yvonne stood up to greet them.

"May I help you?" she said.

"Are you Yvonne Williams?" asked the dark-suited woman.

"Yes."

Harlan Ames planted both hands flat on the conference table, glaring at his security team.

"Who are these people?" he barked.

The woman stepped forward quickly and nodded at him.

"Mr. Ames, I'm Special Agent Francina Dawson, Federal Bureau of Investigation," she said. Her speaking style was very clipped and formal. "I'll be in charge of the investigation into the disappearance of Mr. Thomas Swift." Then she gestured to each of the three men with her. "This is Agent Fitzpatrick, Agent Bartley, and Agent Bogenn. They'll be posted here, effective immediately."

"Posted?" repeated Harlan Ames.

"Yes," said Agent Dawson. "And I know you'll give them your fullest cooperation."

Harlan was speechless.

Agent Dawson faced my mother next. "I'm sorry, Mrs. Swift," she said, giving a curt bow. "I'll need to speak with you in private this afternoon. Can you come down to the Federal Building at around three o'clock?"

Mom looked a little dazed. "Yes, I . . . I suppose so."

"Good," said Agent Dawson abruptly. Then she turned to face me. "And you're Tom Swift, the son?"

"Yes, ma'am," I said.

The FBI agent flipped open a small PDA unit and punched a button on it. "You were at the scene of the disappearance, correct?"

"He didn't *disappear*," I said. "He was kidnapped. And yes, I was there."

"In what capacity?"

"As a son," I answered.

Agent Dawson frowned. "I don't understand."

"I was hiking with my father. You know, as . . . father and son."

"For what purpose?"

I tried not to scoff. "For, like . . . fun?"

"So you're saying there was no official purpose to your outing other than . . . family enjoyment?"

"That's correct, Agent Dawson."

"You were just hiking?"

"In a nutshell," I said.

She whipped out a small pencil-like stylus and started tapping it on the PDA screen. She handled it awkwardly, frowning and squinting at the display. She glanced up and caught my amused look, then said, "I hate this thing."

I didn't respond. She was starting to bug me.

"So I'm looking at your statements in the police report, Mr. Swift," said Agent Dawson. She squinted as she read. Her eyebrows suddenly lifted. "There was a woman, you say?" She gave me a hard look. "Are you sure?"

"I'm absolutely sure."

"She was in charge?" said Dawson.

"Without a doubt. She was giving the orders, and the others were jumping."

Dawson nodded. "Interesting."

"How so?" I asked.

"Well, for one, it will be interesting to match wits with another woman."

"What difference does it make?" blurted Sandy.

My sister isn't always the most tactful person, but in this case I had to agree. Man or woman . . . who cared? Somebody kidnapped my dad.

Agent Dawson smiled at Sandy, but her eyes flashed a glint of irritation.

"You're right," said Dawson. "It makes no difference." She turned abruptly to Harlan Ames. "Mr. Ames, I'm going to ask you to give us full access to your internal communications database."

Harlan frowned. "Why?"

"Well, we have all sorts of reasons," replied Agent Dawson with an edge. "None of which are your business."

The Swift security head stood up. He leaned forward on the table, his laserlike glare burning into Agent Dawson.

"Young lady," he said. "I spent twenty years in the field for the Bureau. I've stood in your place many times. I assure you there will be no security breach through me. And my full security team is at your disposal." He nodded at the Swift security guards by the door. "I have good people. The best, in fact. My cyber-security unit rivals anything you have in your regional field office, believe me. Our internal investigation is already well under way, so maybe we can coordinate and get your team up to speed quickly on what we know."

"I'm shutting down your internal investigation," said Agent Dawson. "Effective immediately."

Harlan, his face reddening, waited several seconds before replying. "And why is that?" he asked through tight teeth.

Agent Dawson took a step toward an empty chair at the table.

"May I sit down?" she asked.

Yvonne Williams said, "Of course."

Agent Dawson slipped into the chair and folded her hands on the table. "Let me be frank," she said. "We have every reason to believe that Mr. Swift's disappearance was an inside job."

I exchanged a stunned look with Sandy. She suddenly slapped the table.

"You're saying . . . somebody *here* did it?" she said. "That's, like, totally whacked!"

Agent Dawson gave her a dark look. Then she turned to Yvonne Williams. "We shouldn't discuss the tactical situation in front of the children."

"He's my dad!" said Sandy.

"Let's go, Sandy," said my mother abruptly. She pushed back from the table and got up to leave. "Yvonne, we'll wait in your office."

Yvonne nodded. "Mrs. Henderson, could you escort Mary and Sandy, please?"

"Gladly," said Mrs. Henderson.

As they left the room, I watched Agent Dawson peck at her PDA with the stylus. She seemed exasperated by the device, or maybe by what she was seeing on-screen. Then I glanced at the other agents. All three were very calm and professional.

When the door closed behind Mrs. Henderson, Agent Dawson looked up and said, "There are indications that inside cooperation made the kidnapping possible. We believe somebody made privileged information about Mr. Swift and his plans available to the perpetrators."

Here I noticed that Agents Bogenn, Bartley, and Fitzpatrick were scanning the people in the room. I got the uncomfortable feeling we were all being observed by a trio of human lie detectors.

"Everyone in this company, including those of you in this room, is officially under the umbrella of suspicion, which is quite broad at this early point." She turned to me. "Except for you, of course."

"Are you sure?" I said. I meant it to be, well, *slightly* sarcastic. But Agent Dawson just nodded.

"Yes, you're free to go, for now," she said. "But I'd like to speak to you later about your recollections of the incident in question."

"Of course, Agent Dawson," I said.

"Oh, one other thing, Mr. Swift." She gave me a classic schoolteacher's look. "On the way here I read a lengthy dossier on some of your recent sleuthing exploits. Impressive detective skills—but please note that impeding a federal investigation is a federal crime. The penalty is steep." She smiled pleasantly. "Even for a minor."

I nodded. "I understand."

She didn't seem satisfied with my answer. She leaned toward me and said, "I know you're concerned about your father. But no Hardy Boys stuff . . . understand? If you make any attempt to investigate this case, I'll be very angry."

I smiled back pleasantly. "Why would I do something like that?"

"I'm glad we understand each other," said Agent Dawson. "Now . . . I have some business to attend to with these people here, so I'd appreciate it if you'd wait for me in the lobby." She turned to Yvonne Williams, clearly finished with me.

As I left the room, I heard Agent Dawson saying, "Ms. Williams, you have the right to remain silent. Anything you say can and will be used against you in a court of law . . ."

3

A Worm and a Mole

My meeting later with Special Agent Dawson was uneventful. She pushed me hard to recall every detail about the masked woman who led the kidnapping team. Her questioning about the leader was so intense, I got the feeling Francina Dawson was getting obsessed with finding her female counterpart on the bad guys' team. She made me repeat every detail I could remember about the woman with the Southern accent.

Afterward, I got onto the elevator and rode to the top floor, where I knew Mom and Sandy were waiting in Yvonne Williams's office. When the elevator door slid open, Sandy was standing there waiting.

"They told me you were coming," she said.

"Yeah. What's up?"

Sandy stepped into the elevator and punched the "Floor: Sub 5" button. Several Swift laboratories and workshops were located underground in a series of highly secure subbasements. As the doors closed, she turned to me. "You're going to look for Dad, right?"

I nodded. "Of course I am."

"But Agent Dawson told you not to, right?"

I nodded again. "Right."

She got a sly look on her face. "Suppose I wanted to join you?"

I shook my head. "No."

"Listen," she said. "He's my dad too. And I'm smarter than you are."

I raised my eyebrows. "Really?"

"Without a doubt," she said with a little grin. "And if you try to look for him without my help, I'll . . . I'll rat you out to the feds." She paused for a second, thinking. Then she added, "Plus I'll tell Mom about that time you snuck out after midnight and took the Speedster to the county highway for power-slide testing."

"Wow," I said. "You'd blackmail your own brother?"

26

"Yes."

I nodded, trying not to smile. "Well, if you feel that strongly about it . . ."

"I do," she said. And I could see in Sandy's suddenly intense eyes that she was not kidding. "And I know *exactly* where to begin our investigation."

I glanced at the lit elevator button for the fifth floor underground.

"Victor's lab," I said.

"Am I right?" she asked.

I grinned. "Yes, you're right." This is exactly where I'd planned to get started as well.

"So is it a deal?" asked Sandy.

I stuck out my hand. "Deal."

Dr. Victor Rashid was one of the smartest people in the world; I was absolutely sure of that. He was in his early sixties, gaunt and frail—arms so thin it seemed you'd snap them off if you shook his hand too hard. But if you talked to Victor for about five minutes, his intelligence made him grow before your very eyes, as if his brain were inflating the muscles beneath his dark, leathery skin.

Okay, maybe that sounds weird. But Victor

Rashid's brain was definitely one of the most powerful things ever.

"Thomas!" he called from across his office with his light, vaguely Arabic accent. "And Sandra, too!" He hurried over to us, his face an uncharacteristic mask of grief. "I am so upset about your father, so upset. This is terrible news. I could not sleep last night, Thomas." He flung a bony arm around each of us. "I don't know what to say."

"We're okay, Victor," said Sandy. "Because we're going to find him."

"You are?" he asked. He looked at me.

I nodded. "With your help, maybe," I said.

Victor was Swift's lab director and head scientist. His own lab and offices occupied the entire fifth-floor subbasement. While five underground floors may seem like an unhealthy and perhaps even grim setup, the Swift Tower was designed to be a healthy work space. Full-spectrum lamps glowed like morning sunlight through rice-paper "windows" on lab walls; the effect was warm, inviting, even stimulating. And a revolutionary airflow system designed by Dr. Rashid himself kept a constant, barely perceptible "breeze" of pure ionized air moving through the lower levels at all times.

"Well, then," said Victor, rubbing his hands together. "Let's get started. How can I help you?"

"First, what's Dad been working on lately?" I asked.

Victor Rashid's eyes lit up. "Ah!" he said. "Come with me."

He led us down a corridor past several smaller lab/workshops where prototypes of Swift inventions sat in various states of assembly: a holographic 3-D television set, a foldable airplane with collapsible wings, a personal minisubmarine disguised as a shark, et cetera. Wild stuff.

"As you can see," said Dr. Rashid, "we have many things in the works. But your father has been focusing on a pet project. A rather ambitious one, as always."

He waved a pass card in front of an electronic reader at a large metal security door. The door clicked, and then Dr. Rashid opened it. We stepped into a larger lab with a fantastic array of laser cutters, machining tools, wires, electronic modules, and creepy-looking robotic assembly units. In the center of the room on a raised platform sat a large vehicle,

roughly the size and shape of a small airplane fuselage, with an enormous drill-shaped nose cone.

"Meet the Mega-Worm," said Dr. Rashid.

"What is it, Victor?" asked Sandy, wide-eyed.

"An industrial boring machine," replied Dr. Rashid.
"She's twenty feet long, watertight, weighs more
than four tons—indeed, the drill bit alone weighs
more than two thousand pounds. At top speed she
can burrow nearly four hundred feet an hour through
solid rock. We think it can drill fairly large tunnels
down to depths of approximately two hundred feet,
depending on the soil makeup."

I was stunned. All I could say was, *"Whoa!"*

"Subway construction, water management,
mining—all of these industries will be revolution-
ized," added Dr. Rashid. "And of course, being a
scientist, I envision the scientific uses. Imagine the
exploration it makes possible!"

Sandy pointed across the room. "What's that over
there?" she asked. "It looks the same, but smaller."

Dr. Rashid led us across the lab. "Yes, that is the
Mini-Worm," he said. "Our prototype."

Dr. Rashid ran through the Mini-Worms specs: a
mere eight feet long, under a thousand pounds, but

a much faster-turning drill mechanism let it exceed the burrowing pace of its larger sibling, the Mega-Worm.

"I assume the prototype works," I said, admiring it.

"Oh yes, it tested quite well," said Dr. Rashid. "Beyond our wildest hopes, actually. But we haven't yet field-tested the Mega-Worm; it has bugs still." Then he gave me a dark look. "You don't think our work on these machines has anything to do with Dr. Swift's abduction, do you?"

I shrugged. "At this point we know almost nothing," I said. "I just figure we'd better assume Dad's kidnappers know a lot about him and his work, and maybe have some motive other than just ransom money."

"Has there been a ransom request?"

"No," I said. "We've heard nothing."

Dr. Rashid looked terrible. He slumped down into a chair at a worktable. "Mr. Swift . . . your father . . . is a visionary man," he said. "The work he's done . . . and the work he inspires us to do here, every day." He shook his head. "He is an irreplaceable figure."

I put my hand on the scientist's tiny shoulder.

"Victor, I swear we'll get him back," I said.

"What are the authorities doing?" he asked.

"Well, right now the FBI is upstairs trying to put the clamps on Harlan's internal investigation."

Dr. Rashid smiled. "Knowing Harlan Ames, they will be most unsuccessful in that endeavor."

Sandy and I both chuckled. I said, "The lead agent warned me off the case as well."

"Another foolish mistake," said Dr. Rashid with a sad smile.

Later that evening Sandy and I spent a couple of hours sitting in Mom's art studio going over everything we knew (which wasn't much) about the case. Half-finished clay sculptures leaned over our shoulders, listening in: a coyote half raised on hind legs, a barn owl in repose, a possum on a branch. Mom loved nature, and most of her work was realistic portrayals of wildlife. I don't want to brag, but the name Mary Nestor Smith is a celebrated one in the art world. Her studio, an amazing glass dome over the garage, is world famous.

"It seems odd that there's been no contact," I said. "It's been more than twenty-four hours."

"I guess they're patient types," said Sandy.

Neither one of us spoke the obvious worst case—that the kidnappers weren't interested in money or demands; they just wanted Thomas Swift Sr. removed from the scene. If that was the case, Dad may have come to harm.

"Run through everything that happened out there one more time," said Sandy.

I glanced at her. She was taking meticulous notes by hand in a composition notebook. Sandy and I had a pretty good brother-sister relationship, I guess. We weren't exactly best friends, and she could be annoying sometimes. But the girl was amazing, without a doubt. She had a photographic memory, and her skill at doing mathematical calculations in her head was freaky. Like me, she had her own lab. But her experiments focused on pure science instead of the practical applications and gadgets I liked to tinker with.

And her relentless determination, in this case, would be an asset, I figured.

Suddenly my cell phone beeped. I looked at the incoming number in the display, then eagerly flipped open the phone.

"Dude!" I said into the phone.

"Did you find him yet?" blurted a boy's voice.

"Not yet," I replied. "No word yet."

Bud Barclay was my best friend and had been since first grade when we met. An aspiring journalist, he was in Chicago doing a four-week summer internship with the city's major newspaper.

"I just talked to my mom," he said, sounding shaken. "She . . . she just saw the Shopton paper this morning, and called me right away."

"It's a mess, dude," I said, feeling a wave of sorrow for the first time since the incident. Something about Bud's voice got to me.

"Are you okay?" asked Bud.

"I'm worried," I said. "The police wanted to keep things quiet at first. But . . ."

"But a huge fireball rising from the slopes of Mount Shopton is hard to keep on the down low," interjected Bud. "Dang, my mom says the explosion rattled her office window downtown."

"It *was* huge," I agreed.

"Is Casmir okay?"

"Yeah, he's a beast," I said. "I talked to him this morning. He blames himself, of course. But he took a wicked shot. He's lucky he's alive."

"I want to come home and help you, man," said Bud.

"No, no . . . not yet. There's nothing you can do right now. But thanks for calling, man." I took a deep breath and added, "How's the big city?"

"Big," answered Bud. "Extremely big. It has big shoulders, Chicago does."

"Are you having fun?"

Bud paused. "I was until today," he said. "It's hard to have fun when your best bud is . . . you know . . ."

"Yeah," I said. "I know."

"Keep me posted. I'll check in again tomorrow. Peace."

"Peace," I said, and hung up.

I looked over at Sandy. She had several pages of notes scribbled already. She looked up at me and said, "Let's find out if anybody else is developing a heavy-duty boring machine."

"Good idea," I said. "Q.U.I.P.?"

"I exist to do your bidding," chirped my wrist unit.

I smiled. Q.U.I.P.'s "personality," as it were, was remarkably consistent. The programming allowed him to develop a dynamic, constantly evolving self, and he could be all business when that function was required. But overall, Q.U.I.P.'s "self" was that of a teenage class clown.

"Get online with your search engine," I said. "Find out if any known industrial entity admits that it has a drilling or boring or tunneling vehicle in any state of development. Take your time."

"I did," said Q.U.I.P. "I found two."

"You're . . . already done?"

"Sorry it took so long," he said. "But you told me to take my time."

I grinned. "Okay, who's building a worm?"

"One is Ulansky Oil and Gas, based in Russia," said Q.U.I.P. "Their mobile driller is already on the market, but it's not strictly a 'worm' like the Swift vehicle you described. It has a manned compartment, and it does bore into the ground, but only vertically. Its purpose is to create a housing shaft for oil-extraction equipment." Q.U.I.P. paused. "By the way, I've got an itch."

"Is that right?" I replied.

"Yes," said Q.U.I.P. "Something is bugging me."

Sandy laughed at this. "You crack me up, Q.U.I.P.," she said.

"I'm so happy I do," he replied, "but I'm not kidding. I sense something strange in my head."

I slipped the wrist unit off and examined it. "Hmmm," I said. "One of the casing screws is gouged pretty badly." I whipped out a micro-tool set from one of the pockets on my cargo shorts and used a miniscrewdriver to unscrew the casing. As I worked, I asked, "Who's the other company?"

"Foger Utility Group," said Q.U.I.P.

I dropped the two screws, the watch casing, and the screwdriver as Sandy and I both shouted, "*What?*"

As I scrambled for the dropped stuff, Q.U.I.P. said, "Well, boss, according to the FUG corporate press release I'm reading, they built a borer prototype called the Mole One. This vehicle is FUG's entry in competition for a hundred-million-dollar contract with the U.S. Department of Energy."

"Holy cow," I said. "Does the press release list the other corporate competitors?"

"No," replied Q.U.I.P.

Sandy abruptly whipped out her cell phone. "I'll bet you a hundred million bucks that Swift Enterprises is one of them," she said. "I'll give Victor a call."

As she punched in Victor's phone number, I glanced into the back of my wrist unit. An unfamiliar capsule—a tiny disk about the size of an aspirin tablet, but flatter—was jammed into a small depression in the electronics. I started to dig it out with the miniscrewdriver.

"You're tickling me, boss," said Q.U.I.P.

The disk popped out into the palm of my hand.

"What the donkey is this?" I asked.

"Hey, Victor, quick question," said Sandy into her phone. "Is the Mega-Worm project part of some bid for a big government contract with the Department of Energy or something?" She listened to Dr. Rashid's reply.

I examined the tiny capsule; it looked metallic, perforated with dozens of tiny holes. I decided to scan it and then maybe slice it apart with a laser cutter in my lab.

Sandy said, "Okay, yeah, that's what we thought. And we're bidding against FUG, right?" She listened again. "That's very interesting, Victor. Yes, I'll tell Tom. Okay, thanks very much. Bye."

"Tell me what?" I asked, slipping the metal capsule into my pocket.

Sandy's eyes were aglow. "No surprise, we're bidding against FUG for the government contract," she said. "And it's just us and them—the Mega-Worm versus the Mole One. There are no other corporate bidders." She slipped her phone into her pocket. "But something's up, Tom."

The excitement in her eyes was unmistakable. "Well, what is it?" I asked.

"Victor just talked to Harlan Ames," she replied. "The FBI has scheduled a press conference for eight o'clock tomorrow morning, downtown at the Federal Building."

"To announce what?" I asked.

"Victor doesn't know exactly," said Sandy. "But he says Agent Dawson told Harlan he's no longer under her 'umbrella of suspicion.' In fact, nobody at Swift Enterprises is any longer considered a suspect."

I jumped to my feet. "Sounds like the FBI got a break in the case."

Sandy glanced up at Mom's coyote sculpture-in-progress leering down at her. "Dang," she said, "maybe I was wrong about Special Agent Dawson." She closed her notebook. "I hate being wrong."

I grinned. "Hey, I'd rather be wrong if it means the

FBI finds the goons and we get Dad back."

Sandy nodded. "Let's go tell Mom!" she said, heading for the studio's exit elevator.

We found Mom on the phone in the kitchen. Her eyes were bright—and I guessed correctly that she was speaking with someone about the FBI press conference. When she hung up, she announced we were invited to be at the Federal Building at seven forty-five the next morning.

Then we broke out the milk and Girl Scout cookies.

It was going to be a long night.

The Text

At 7:58 a.m. the next morning, I sat in the Federal Building media room in a row of chairs with Mom, Sandy, Yvonne Williams, Harlan Ames, and several other executive staff members from Swift Enterprises. Quite a few reporters and several camera crews were set up behind us. The excitement in the room was palpable. But Yvonne was not happy.

"Why wouldn't Agent Dawson brief us before putting on this little show?" she said.

Harlan Ames nodded grimly. "I would never have pulled a stunt like this without meeting with the family first," he said. "This isn't standard operating procedure for the Bureau—not when I was there, anyway."

My mom calmly touched Harlan's shoulder. "Let's

give Agent Dawson the benefit of the doubt on this one," she said. "She must have her reasons."

Right on time at eight a.m., the side doors abruptly flew open and Agent Dawson strode across the front of the room, carrying a briefcase in one hand and a single sheet of paper in the other. She was followed by Agents Fitzpatrick, Bogenn, and Bartley. As she stepped up to the podium and adjusted the microphone, cameras behind us whirred and clicked, snapping photo after photo. The murmuring rose in volume all around us, but then the room hushed as Agent Dawson laid the sheet of paper on the podium and began to speak.

"Good morning, everyone, and thank you for being here," she said. "I'm Special Agent Francina Dawson, Federal Bureau of Investigation. I'm going to read a short statement, then I'll take questions." She looked down at the sheet on the podium. "At nine thirty-three p.m. last night, we took a suspect in the Thomas Swift kidnapping case into custody at his residence in north Shopton. Randall Foger offered no resistance and spent the night in a holding cell here at the Federal Building."

The crowd gasped as one, and chatter rose. But of

course, neither Sandy nor I were very surprised. After learning about the industrial competition between SE and FUG on the lucrative super-drilling-vehicle contract, it made some sense. But I still couldn't believe Mr. Foger would go that far for the sake of a federal contract.

Agent Dawson continued her statement, revealing a few details of the government contract competition. Then she dropped the bombshell.

"Our preliminary investigation uncovered some incriminating evidence on Mr. Foger's personal computers, both at his home and in his Foger Utility Group office."

"What sort of evidence?" blurted a reporter.

Agent Dawson looked up. "Confidential plans and blueprints of a Swift Enterprises project that was in direct competition with Mr. Foger's project," she said. "A fairly blatant case of industrial espionage."

Again the press room exploded in a cacophony of voices calling out questions.

"What was Randall Foger's response?" cried out a reporter. "Do you have a confession?"

"No confession," said Agent Dawson. "Mr. Foger denied his involvement in any of these matters, then on advice of counsel, he refused to speak further."

"What about the kidnapping?" shouted a reporter. "What evidence links Foger to the Swift disappearance?"

"I can't comment on that yet," said Agent Dawson.

"What about the explosion site?" called another reporter. "Anything linked to that? The Jeep?"

"No comment," said Agent Dawson. She held up her hands to quiet the crowd. "Any other questions?"

The press conference went on a few more minutes, with Agent Dawson and her cohorts answering a few questions. Most of their replies, however, were variations of the "I can't comment on that at this time" response. Then Agent Dawson concluded the proceeding.

"We will be speaking with Swift family members and company employees upstairs in the FBI offices immediately following this press conference," she said. She nodded at Mom and Yvonne, who sat side by side. "The family and company may have statements to make to you after those meetings. Or they may not. It's their prerogative. Thank you, ladies and gentlemen. That will be all."

And she strode out of the room.

Harlan Ames leaned forward and gazed down the row toward Mom, Sandy, and me. "I think she enjoyed her little production," he said with a hint of disdain. "Now let's go see if there's any meat in the sandwich."

Then we all stood to head upstairs.

"Naturally, Mr. Foger insists he had nothing to do with Mr. Swift's abduction," said Agent Dawson, sipping on an herbal tea drink.

We sat in a small conference room in the Federal Building, a tall structure that housed the chambers of the U.S. District Court plus offices for several federal departments, including the FBI. The basement floor consisted of holding cells for federal prisoners appearing in trials. Randall Foger now occupied one of those cells.

I poked at a stale scone I'd been offered by a friendly assistant at the FBI reception desk.

"Agent Dawson," I said, "I can see why FUG's involvement seems logical, given the bad blood between the two companies over the years."

"Bad blood?" chuckled Agent Dawson. "Yes, I'll say."

She lifted a thick folder sitting in front of her. "I've never seen such a bitter, personal corporate rivalry." She flipped open the folder and started reading some notes jotted on the top document. "Randall Foger and Thomas Swift Sr., business partners twenty-five years ago. Partnership quickly foundered on widely divergent business interests."

"Yeah," blurted Sandy. "Like, Foger wanted to cheat, and Dad didn't."

I had to grin at Sandy. Among other things, Randall Foger had wanted to aggressively market an experimental, new jet engine that Dad considered unsafe. Dad had also caught Foger using Swift-designed optical technology to spy on competitors and threatened to expose his unethical partner unless he let Dad buy out Foger's half of the company.

"We're aware of Mr. Foger's past," sniffed Agent Dawson in her impeccable manner.

She read more of her notes. The story was that Randall Foger has been playing dirty since the day he incorporated Foger Utility Group in Shopton to compete with his old company, now renamed Swift Enterprises. FUG has a long history of sabotage and espionage and even blackmail directed at Swift.

Foger has never thought twice about trying unethical or even dangerous activities in the name of corporate progress. He was once quoted as saying, "My only social responsibility is profit." But his cleverness in covering his tracks has kept FUG's record remarkably clean. He always uses intermediaries to do the dirty work.

"So again," I said, "my point is that it would seem awfully risky for FUG to try something as blatant as this, just for the sake of some corporate advantage in bidding for a contract."

"Yes, Randall's too smart to be directly involved in kidnapping a rival," grumbled Harlan Ames, staring into his coffee cup. "Don't get me wrong—I despise the man. But he's not stupid enough to be *this* obvious."

Agent Dawson cleared her throat.

"Mr. Ames, we do have physical evidence from the scene that suggests a connection between the kidnappers and Foger Utility Group," she said. "In fact, some of our data indicates the direct, personal involvement of Mr. Foger himself in the planning."

Harlan squinted at her. "I'd like to see that evidence," he said skeptically.

Agent Dawson's cold eyes didn't match her warm smile. "Too bad you're no longer with the Bureau," she said to Harlan. "I'd love to share our findings."

Now she stood up and looked directly at Harlan.

"Mr. Ames," she said, "have you checked your personal bank account in the past forty-eight hours?"

Harlan frowned. "No," he said. "Why?"

"Well, we have," said Agent Dawson.

She gestured toward one of her cohorts, Agent Bartley, a stocky man with glasses. He stepped forward and flipped open a binder in his hands.

"Mr. Ames," he said, "we're wondering about the nature of these two electronic deposits, both quite large, made directly into your National Bank checking account in the past two days."

Harlan gripped the armrests of his chair.

"What are you talking about?" he said.

"One deposit went into your account two days ago, in the amount of fifty thousand dollars," said Agent Bartley, glancing down at his binder. "Another went in last night . . . another fifty thousand." The agent gave Harlan a cynical look. "Gee, Mr. Ames, that's a lot of money."

Harlan stood up slowly. His anger was just barely

under control. He looked at Yvonne Williams, who looked ill.

"This is a setup," he said.

Yvonne just nodded at him.

"Maybe," said Agent Dawson, holding her teacup daintily. "But how else could Randall Foger obtain blueprints for a top-secret Swift project? Or highly sensitive information about Mr. Swift's movements in a wilderness area such as Theodore Roosevelt State Park—a *perfect* area to stage a kidnapping, by the way."

"Are you kidding?" exploded Harlan. "Do you think I would be *stupid* enough to do that? Let some criminal transfer large sums of money directly into my private bank account?"

Agent Dawson just shrugged. I knew her smug, self-satisfied look was a calculated one. She was trying to bait Harlan's anger and get him to slip.

I couldn't take it anymore. "This is insane," I suddenly said.

Everybody looked at me. I glared at Agent Dawson.

Look, sometimes you just have to trust your basic instinct. I'd known Harlan Ames for years; I'd talked to Dad about Harlan many times. Nobody was more trustworthy than Harlan. Nobody was more loyal. Nobody had more personal integrity. Whoever decided to frame an insider had made a foolish choice in selecting Harlan Ames. Nobody at Swift Enterprises or in the Swift family would believe Harlan had betrayed my father for a few bucks. It was ludicrous.

"Harlan wouldn't do this in a million years," I said to Dawson. "You should be tracking the money source. Focus on *that*, not on the place where it ended up. Anybody can find a bank account number and rig a money wire transfer into it."

Harlan gave me a grateful look. "Exactly," he said.

Agent Dawson's eyes flashed with anger as she turned to me. But she kept her voice steady as she said, "Mr. Swift, I can appreciate your sentiments. But you can be sure that the FBI knows a few things about banking and wire transfers, and we don't need lectures on the subject from distraught sixteen-year-old boys."

Apparently this woman was a master at baiting anger. So I decided to play her game.

"I'm not lecturing you, Agent Dawson," I said. "I'm just pointing out the obvious."

Agent Dawson turned to her trio of agents and said, "Please re-advise Mr. Ames of his Miranda rights. Then place Mr. Ames in federal custody."

I turned to Harlan. "Don't worry," I said. "We'll get you cleared."

Harlan took a deep breath, then smiled.

He glanced over at Agent Dawson and said, "Well, Tom, judging from the performance so far, I expect to be out by this evening."

Agent Dawson shot to her feet and strode quickly to the door of the conference room. Before she stepped outside, she turned to give me a crooked smile.

"Please, Thomas, remember what I said about interfering with a federal investigation," she said. "When we find your father—and rest assured that we *will*—I would hate for his homecoming to be marred by your incarceration in a juvenile detention center."

This was too much for Mom.

She slapped the table and said, "That's *quite* enough, Agent Dawson! I'll not have you threatening my son while his father is a *kidnap victim*."

Agent Dawson looked chastened a bit. She nodded

and said, "I am sorry, Mrs. Swift. But please encourage your son to keep his infamous sleuthing and *gadgetry* out of this investigation."

She practically spit out "gadgetry," as if it were a dirty word. Then she spun and exited the room.

Agent Fitzpatrick approached my mother. "I'm sorry, Mrs. Swift," he said. "We have to escort you and your family home now. We need you there in case the kidnappers try to make contact with ransom or other demands."

"I understand," she said, standing. "Tom? Sandy?"

Sandy and I left the room with her. Yvonne Williams came with us. As I left, I glanced back sadly at Harlan Ames. The other two agents had stepped up on either side of him, preparing for a search as they read him his rights.

The door clunked shut behind me.

Suddenly my cell phone buzzed. It was an incoming text message. I flipped it open—and nearly tripped, I was so stunned at who the sender was.

I quickly punched the read button and saw this text: PLS MEET ME ASAP ANYWHERE, NEED HELP.

The message was from Andy Foger.

An Unlikely Alliance

Shopton High School was closed down for the summer—for the most part, anyway. Coach Jenkins ran a few summer sports clinics for younger kids out on the fields, and the school's north wing was open for summer school classes. But the grounds were largely deserted in July.

So I arranged to meet Andy Foger, my lifelong nemesis and son of Randall Foger, in the outdoor amphitheater built into the hill behind the gymnasium. It was a quiet, secluded place. Plus we could stand on the stage with a good view in all directions—you know, just in case we were being tailed by federal agents or kidnappers or evil spies or, just, whatever.

I was starting to get paranoid.

My sister was with me. Earlier at the Federal Building, she'd noticed the shocked look on my face at receiving a text from the son of Dad's alleged kidnapper. Sandy, being Sandy, had hounded me unmercifully until I told her who sent the message.

"I'm coming with you," she'd said.

"I'm sure Andy will be thrilled," I'd replied.

"Whatever."

Now we stood on the amphitheater stage. I felt nervous, remembering Special Agent Dawson's warnings against doing any sleuthing on the case. I guess I was supposed to go home and read comic books or something until the adults finished their police work.

Sorry. That's not my style.

After just five minutes or so, we spotted Andy at the top of the bowl-shaped amphitheater. He looked over his shoulder a couple of times as he jogged down the stairs. I guess he was feeling as paranoid as I was.

"Hey, Andy," I called. "What's up?"

He scowled at Sandy as he approached. "What's *she* doing here?"

Sandy folded her arms. "I'm a mole for the feds."

I grinned. "Sandy wants to help," I said, and shrugged at Andy.

"Get rid of her."

"Your dad kidnapped my dad," said Sandy. "So I believe I'll stay."

"He didn't!" said Andy. "Somebody's framing us!"

"How we can we be sure of that?" asked Sandy. "Do you have evidence to clear FUG and your dad?"

Andy shook his head sullenly. "But I have some evidence that nobody else has regarding the kidnappers. I'll share it with you if you agree to help me find the *real* kidnappers."

He looked kind of sheepish saying this. I frowned at him.

"What kind of evidence?" I asked.

"Well, I . . . I have an audio recording."

"Of what?" I asked.

"The incident."

"What incident?"

"The *kidnapping*, you dork," blustered Andy.

I eyed him suspiciously. "How could you have an audio recording of the kidnapping . . . unless you were there?"

Andy just pointed at my wrist.

"I *knew* something was bugging me," chirped Q.U.I.P. from my wrist unit. He chortled at his own pun.

I stared at Andy for a second. Then I remembered the small capsule I'd removed the night before. I'd gotten so caught up in the news of the FBI press conference that I'd decided to postpone disassembly of the mystery capsule until later. Now I knew: It was a bug.

"You bugged my watch," I said. "How?"

Andy smirked proudly. "You shouldn't take it off during PE class, Swift."

"I lock it in my gym locker," I said.

"Yeah, like *that* could stop me," said Andy, rolling his eyes. "Anyway, I've been eavesdropping on your pathetically boring life since the last week of school in May."

My eyes got big. "And you recorded the kidnapping?" I said, getting excited.

Andy nodded. "On Sunday I was taping your hike with your dad, just in case you gave away technical secrets of your new Chameleon Suit. I wanted to rip off your ideas."

Well, one thing you can say about Andy: He's

brutally honest about his lowly behavior. *Like father like son*, I thought. All I could do was shake my head in awe at his total lack of a normal conscience.

"Wow," I said. "Why didn't you notify the police?"

"Are you nuts?" said Andy. "We look guilty enough already. We've already been accused of industrial espionage."

"Ah, I see your point," I said.

"Do you have the recording with you?" asked Sandy.

"Yeah. Wanna hear it?" Andy pulled a small MP3 player from his pocket. "I saved it as an MP3 file and downloaded it onto this."

He plugged a pair of earbuds into the player and handed them to me. Sandy and I each plugged a bud in one ear and listened as Andy played the recording.

It was eerie and, as it progressed, more upsetting than I was prepared for. The background rumbling of the Jeep and the rustling of my camouflage suit as I ran muffled the harsh snarl of the leader's voice. I could barely make out her shouted instructions: "*Forget sonny boy! Ya'll get back in the car! Let's get gone!*" Just seconds later I listened to Casmir's moan as I bent over him. The recording ran all the way to the sudden boom of the explosion, then the arrival of the police unit and the medivac.

When I glanced over at Sandy, tears were rolling down her cheeks. I flung an arm around her.

"Okay, that's enough," I said, handing the earbuds back to Andy.

Andy nodded. "So what can we do with this recording?"

"One answer is, turn it over to the FBI," I said.

"Do you trust them?" asked Andy.

"I'm not sure."

"They *must* be corrupt," he said.

"Why?" asked Sandy, wiping her wet face. "Not everybody's like your family."

This flew right over Andy's head. It was almost amusing how he didn't seem to take it as an insult.

"Well, I'm pretty sure my dad didn't kidnap your dad," he said. "I mean, I was there in the office when Dad heard about it yesterday." Andy squinted one eye, remembering. "He was, like . . . *stunned*."

Sandy and I exchanged a look. Andy actually seemed sincere about this recollection.

"And so if Dad didn't do it," continued Andy, "then

the FBI is either corrupt or tragically wrong."

"Impressive logic," said Sandy.

"I'd go with tragically wrong," I said. Then I told him what happened with Harlan Ames in the Federal Building earlier that morning. Normally I wouldn't share this sort of info with anybody, let alone my worst enemy in town. But these were extraordinary times. "Andy, can you imagine your dad and Harlan Ames in cahoots?"

Andy hooted a harsh laugh. "Heck no! They hate each other's guts!"

Sandy sat down on the stage, staring at the burnished wood floorboards. "In one sense, Agent Dawson is correct," she said.

Andy and I sat down too. "How so?" I asked.

"Well," she said, "unless the FBI is just fabricating evidence, which I highly doubt, then the fact is, *somebody* put a blueprint of the Swift Mega-Worm on Randall Foger's computer, right?"

"Right," I said.

"So who had access to those plans?" asked Sandy.

I shook my head. "I don't know—probably a very small number of people. Those plans are undoubtedly some of the best-guarded documents in company

59

history, given the size of the government contract at stake."

Andy nodded in agreement.

"Same with FUG's Mole One design doc," he said. "Red-level security. Dad says only three people in the entire company have access to the full document, and he's one of them. The rest of the design team sees only CAD/CAM files of the specific component they're working on."

"Would Harlan have access to the Mega-Worm blueprints?" asked Sandy.

"Of course he wouldn't," I replied.

"Yeah, but as head of security, the dude probably knows a lot about your company's network-security software," said Andy.

"Good point," I said. "I'm sure that's what the FBI cyber-crime unit is thinking. But I just cannot believe that Harlan is part of this."

"Well, I know my dad is innocent," said Andy.

"I'm willing to accept that," I said. "But then who got those blueprints? And how did they end up in your dad's computer?"

"Maybe it was, like, a hacker," said Andy. "A really, really *good* hacker."

I had to laugh. "Dude, only a wizard-level hacker could slip through the Swift firewall, steal a highly secure document from our protected network, and *then* hack the FUG network, too, and plant the blueprint in your dad's computer—which is no doubt one of the most secure computers in all of corporate America."

Andy shrugged. "Yeah," he agreed.

"Okay," said Sandy, shifting into Nancy Drew mode. "So then, let's be logical. Who would benefit from this crime? Two major high-tech companies are competing for a three-billion-dollar government contract. The kidnapping and the stolen blueprints combine to knock both companies out of commission, removing both company heads and crippling the Mega-Worm and Mole One projects." She looked from me to Andy. "Very clever, I'd say. Is there a third competitor we don't know about? Somebody who wants the contract so badly they'd sabotage both Swift and FUG with this insanely sinister plan?"

We all thought about this for a moment. Then, slowly, we all shook our heads.

"That just sounds too crazy," I said.

"Yeah, and I've heard of no other bidder on this contract," said Andy.

Sandy took out her cell phone. "I'll check with Victor." A quick call confirmed that no other company was involved in the super-driller competition.

"Okay then," I said, looking at Andy. "So who else would benefit from the suffering of our two companies?"

We mused on this question awhile and came up with no obvious culprit other than possibly The Road Back. But the dangerously goofball radicals at TRB would have taken proud responsibility for the kidnapping long ago, releasing puffed-up statements and long-winded proclamations about the evil of modern technology. So it didn't seem likely that TRB was involved in this one.

"Not to mention that I can't picture TRB with a brand-new Jeep," I said. "Jeeps are evil, right?"

Sandy stood up from the stage. "You know, I have a pretty good audio-tech setup in my lab," she said. "I've been playing with filters and digital enhancement and stuff. Maybe I could filter out the background elements and get a better audio of the Southern woman's voice."

Andy snapped his fingers. "Then we can get a voice match from our voice-ID database," he said.

"What database are you talking about?" I asked.

Andy unleashed his trademark smirk. "FUG has a contract with the CIA," he said with smug pride. "We manage the largest voice-identification database in the world."

"Why doesn't that surprise me?" said Sandy.

"Give me a break," said Andy. "I suppose you're going to say that it's a violation of privacy. Ha!" He jabbed his finger at Sandy. "In this day and age, we can't *afford* privacy."

"Whatever," I said. "So Andy, can you get us a copy of this MP3 file?"

Q.U.I.P. jumped in. "We can make a data transfer right now," he said.

"Right," said Andy. "I'll turn on my player's wireless."

"Let's do it," I said.

Andy quickly uploaded the recording to Q.U.I.P. "As soon as you get the leader's voice filtered out, send the cleaned-up recording to me, and I'll run a database search for a match."

"Okay," I said.

We looked at each other for a second. In a

normal situation, we'd seal the partnership with a handshake.

But Andy just shook his head and said, "I can't believe I'm working with you dorks."

I gave him a little salute.

"We love you too, Andy," I said. "And by the way, if you ever spy on me again, I'll kill you."

Andy grinned. "Fair enough."

We said good-bye and headed back to our opposite ends of the moral spectrum.

Five black sedans plus a couple of police cruisers with lights flashing sat in front of our house when we returned. Obviously, something big was up.

Our meeting with Andy had gotten me thinking about the value of recording certain kinds of events.

"This looks very interesting," I said, checking out the cop cars.

"Maybe there's news," said Sandy.

"Q.U.I.P.?" I called.

"Yo dog," replied Q.U.I.P. "S'up?"

"I have a job for you."

"Lay it on me, bro."

"I want you to make audio recordings of any conversations regarding the kidnapping," I said. "No matter who's talking, okay?"

"Including your family?" asked Q.U.I.P.

"Including everyone," I said.

"Federal authorities, too?"

"*Especially* them," I said. "I want every last shred of this investigation documented."

"Okay," said Q.U.I.P.

Sandy and I approached two uniformed policemen at the front door, who nodded and waved us inside. We found Mom silently crying in the kitchen, surrounded by Agent Dawson and a platoon of dark-suited FBI agents.

"What's going on?" I asked with concern. "What happened?"

Mom looked up with bright, wet eyes.

"I just talked to your dad!" she called out as we rushed in.

Sandy dived into Mom's arms. I grabbed Mom's outstretched hand and looked up at Agent Dawson.

The agent said, "We finally got our ransom demand."

"Who from?" I asked. "Did they identify themselves?"

Agent Dawson shook her head.

"Was it the woman with the Southern accent?" I asked.

"No," said Agent Dawson. "It was a synthetic voice, generated by computer."

I nodded. "Clever," I said. "What did they ask for?"

"Thirty-five million dollars," said Agent Dawson.

6

The Pickup

The kidnappers' ransom delivery plan was simple and ingenious: a midnight drop at the old lighthouse.

The ancient structure stood tall and solitary on a promontory overlooking Shopton Harbor. A single-access road called Stonecliff Drive ran to the light-house along a narrow, rocky peninsula. At one point the road dropped through a cut with cliffs rising on either side.

"You'll find surveillance difficult," I said to Agent Dawson. "And tailing your drop unit will be impossible."

She gave me a look and said, "We're surveying the area, Mr. Swift."

"Well, I grew up here," I said. "I've spent many hours out on that point. Trust me, your backup units won't get in close without being detected."

I got the distinct feeling that Agent Dawson was barely tolerating my presence. But she couldn't just kick me out, because (A) I was the kidnapped man's son, and (B) I was right. The kidnappers were smart, I had no doubt. I wanted to make sure Dawson's crew did nothing stupid in response—nothing that could cause harm to befall my father.

Yvonne Williams entered the kitchen from a back room.

"I've just talked to Jack at the bank," she said. "He'll have all thirty-five million in a satchel by tonight."

I was surprised. "We're delivering actual money?" I asked.

Yvonne looked at Agent Dawson, who was exasperated at her PDA again. "The FBI recommends that we do nothing to jeopardize your father's safety," Yvonne said.

"A fake cash drop could be fatal," said Agent Dawson, looking up from her device with irritation. "We'll recover the money afterward."

Yvonne sat down next to Mom and put a hand on her back. Mom smiled at her.

"Thanks for handling this, Yvonne," said Mom, wiping her eyes. "I'm a wreck."

"No, you're a *rock*," said Yvonne. "You're handling this with remarkable grace."

"So was it smooth with the bank?" asked Mom.

"Very smooth," said Yvonne. "Jack's a good banker, though he's a bit surprised at the lack of demands regarding the physical state of the currency. No request for unmarked bills and so forth."

"I'm sure these people have a way to launder cash," said stocky FBI man, Agent Bartley. "Most likely overseas."

I turned to Special Agent Dawson. "So if Randall Foger is behind this plot, why is it still going forward?"

Agent Dawson narrowed her eyes at me.

"I'm sure the perpetrators are on autopilot right now," she said.

"Why?" I asked.

"Mr. Foger is in custody," interjected Agent Bartley.

"Exactly," said Agent Dawson. "The original purpose—to keep Mr. Swift incapacitated and the Mega-Worm project frozen for FUG—has fallen apart because we exposed it. So now the kidnappers are freelancing."

"How can you be sure?" asked Yvonne Williams.

"Do you really think Randall Foger would tell his field team to keep in constant touch with him and wait for direct orders?" said Agent Dawson. "That's not how these things work."

This disturbed me because it actually made sense. Maybe the kidnappers were acting on their own now. Maybe Andy was wrong about his dad, and Mr. Foger was indeed the mastermind. But our meeting with Andy had me convinced that someone else was behind the whole plot.

"Agent Dawson, how can we be sure my husband is going to be safe?" asked my mom.

"We can't," she replied.

In the awkward silence that followed, I decided to go ahead with my plan.

An hour later, as I sat in my personal lab making last-minute adjustments to my Chameleon Suit, my cell phone rang. I smiled at the sight of the incoming number, a familiar one I hadn't seen in a couple of weeks.

"Yo!" I answered.

No, not "yo" as in "yo, dude!"—but rather "Yo!" as in "Yolanda Aponte!" my other best friend besides

Bud. Like Bud, she'd been away at an organized summer activity—in this case, a computer camp in California's Silicon Valley for young software geniuses.

"I just talked to Bud," she said. "Tom, I'm so sorry."

"Thanks."

"Any news?" she asked.

"Yeah, we finally got a ransom demand," I said. "The FBI is making the drop tonight."

I could hear Yo's gasp. "My gosh, Tom," she said.

I heard a clicking in the phone. I knew what that probably meant.

"I'm sure it will go fine," I said casually.

"Will you go along?" asked Yo.

"Nah, I'd just be in the way," I said. "These guys are professionals. I'll probably wait with my Mom at home or maybe just hang out in my lab."

Yo sighed loudly. "I can't believe this, Tom," she said. "I can't believe this is happening to you."

I could hear the emotion in her voice. Like Bud, she was a great friend.

"How's camp?" I asked.

"Actually kind of boring. I'm not really learning much that I don't already know."

I laughed. "Well, that certainly doesn't surprise me."

"Hang in there, dog boy," she said. "I'll be home next week. I hope I'll be giving your dad a big hug then."

"I'm sure you will, Yo," I said. "The FBI will get him back." I hoped I wasn't overdoing the enthusiasm for Dawson and her wiretapping crew. "Peace."

"Peace," she said, and hung up.

I smiled. It's good to know you have close friends. People who care.

I slipped on my Chameleon Suit.

Midnight at the old lighthouse.

I waited nervously next to a rock outcropping on the narrow peninsula, less than three feet from the edge of Stonecliff Drive. I sat atop my matte black Bombardier Embrio, a single-wheeled, gyroscopically balanced motorbike powered by a noiseless, hydrogen fuel cell.

When I saw the headlights come down the road, I froze.

Slowly the black car trolled past me. I could see Agent Dawson in the driver's seat. She was alone in the car. It was dark, but her face was illuminated by dashboard lights, and she looked very calm. I guess I had to admire her professionalism.

As the car passed just inches from me, I waved.

She didn't see me, of course, thanks to my Chameleon Suit, which I had draped over me and my gyrobike. In the dark against a rock wall, I was entirely invisible.

Dawson's black sedan stopped in front of the lighthouse. She stepped out carrying a small, ordinary-looking black satchel. I aimed my gyrobike's front headlamp directly at Agent Dawson.

Then I turned it out.

I shined it *directly* on the doorway area of the lighthouse. But Agent Dawson didn't see a thing, because the light was infrared, invisible to the naked eye. However, I flipped down a pair of ambient-light-collector goggles on my crash helmet, and suddenly the scene before me was as bright as day. I was amazed at the high resolution of the image.

Dawson placed the package near the front door, which was boarded up. The old place had been deserted for years—as far back in my boyhood as I could remember. She looked around coolly and then glided back to her sedan. Without hesitation, she turned the car around and cruised slowly past me again.

As Agent Dawson's sedan approached, she glanced out the driver's-side window, staring straight at me! I fought the urge to flee. It was eerie, but I could tell by her blank look I was still invisible. Then Dawson turned to face straight down the road again.

As she passed, a big smile grew on her face—from the exhilaration of making the drop, I figured.

As the car moved down the rutted lane, I slowly walked my Embrio toward the lighthouse, keeping to the roadside shadows. I knew that two FBI stealth helicopters hovered silently in the distance, about half a mile to the south, waiting to zoom in at the first sign of movement near the lighthouse. I stopped within twenty yards of the satchel on the doorstep. *Close enough*, I thought.

Then I waited.

And waited . . . and waited.

Almost half an hour later, at 12:28 a.m. . . . I was *still* waiting.

Even in July the sea breeze off the point was chilly. I was glad I had the Chameleon Suit draped over me. I hoped my mother hadn't buzzed my lab looking for me, since I'd been out over ninety minutes now.

But I figured she'd be sitting with Yvonne and Sandy and an FBI agent or two, waiting for reports from the pickup and exchange.

I checked my watch—12:31 a.m.

Hmmm. I began to wonder if maybe the kidnappers were technically sophisticated enough to have thermal scanners. My body warmth would show up on a scan and scare them away from making the pickup. But just as I started to think about heading home, I heard a small motor cough to life nearby.

I turned my Embrio's headlamp toward the sound.

Suddenly a rock near the cliff's edge collapsed! I took a closer look. The "rock" was actually a camouflaged tarpaulin . . . and a black-clad figure on a small black motorbike emerged from it. I fired up my Embrio's motor; its hydrogen hum was as quiet as a whisper.

The black motorbike zipped to the lighthouse door and the rider scooped up the satchel. Then he sped off down Stonecliff Drive, moving fast. I squeezed the acceleration trigger on the Embrio's left handlebar. Using only my infrared lights, to remain stealthy, I fell in behind.

Wow! He was moving fast. I could see the motorbike quite clearly via my goggles, but the way he was driving, I feared he might give me the slip. So I decided to make sure I didn't lose him.

"Q.U.I.P.!" I said quietly. "Activate the GPS targeting system."

"*Roger* that, Blue Leader," replied Q.U.I.P. in a deep voice, sounding like a jet fighter pilot. I had an earphone plugged into the wrist unit so only I could hear him. "Acquiring target lock on bogey at twelve o'clock."

Seconds later I heard a beeping sound.

"Blue Leader, we have target lock . . . *now*," said Q.U.I.P.

I heard a quick *whizzzzz!* and saw a brief spark of light shoot off my Embrio's fender assembly.

Then, in my ear, Q.U.I.P. barked, "That's a hit! The bogey is tagged, repeat, *the bogey is tagged*, over."

"Nice shot, dude," I said.

Q.U.I.P. had just used a minilauncher to fire a magnetic GPS projectile called a "tag" at the fleeing motorbike. The homing device hit and attached inconspicuously to the rear fender of the "bogey" and began sending signals to a GPS locator monitored by Q.U.I.P. Technically known as a "tagging and tracking pursuit management system," this same system was being used by police units to make car chases easier and less dangerous. If you lose visual contact with the bogey, you can track it easily with the locator.

It came in handy almost immediately as the road dropped down from the lighthouse promontory and split at the base of the peninsula. When I reached the split, I skidded to a halt; I couldn't see the motorbike.

"Which way?" I called.

"Left," said Q.U.I.P. "Toward the harbor."

I squeezed the acceleration trigger again, and the Embrio rocked back. The gyroscopic balance was incredibly smooth and controlled. I couldn't believe I was traveling on a single wheel. I banked around a sharp turn and caught a glimpse of the motorbike on a curve below.

"Surely the FBI surveillance units saw this guy make the pickup," I said to Q.U.I.P. "Where are the pursuit helicopters?"

"I'm monitoring their field frequency," replied Q.U.I.P. "There seems to be some confusion in their deployment." He paused a second. "Okay, they're on the other side of the peninsula."

"The wrong side, you mean," I said, gritting my teeth.

I lost sight of the motorbike on another curve, but as I rounded the bend, I saw it again, clear as day with my infrared headlamps. It was slowing down along a stretch of shoreline near the water, so I did too.

Then the bike stopped. The rider turned his head and looked toward the water.

I looked too.

"Boss, there's a boat," said Q.U.I.P.

Just as he said it, I heard the outboard motor. Then I saw a slick, streamlined speedboat moving parallel to the shore. Suddenly the black motorbike revved its engine loudly. The rider popped the clutch and the bike lurched straight toward the harbor. It hit a small ramp, going at high speed . . . and then lifted up majestically over the water.

It hit the water and kicked up a fantail splash.

I watched helplessly as the rider bobbed to the surface and stroked powerfully to the speedboat. He flung the black satchel over the gunwale. Then two black-clad figures reached down and hauled him onboard.

I could see it all quite clearly.

"Q.U.I.P., we've got to contact the FBI," I said quickly. "Can you patch me into their field frequency?"

"Already done," said Q.U.I.P. "Go ahead."

The speedboat roared off up the shoreline, then abruptly veered out into a cluster of islands.

"Breaker, breaker, this is Tom Swift, calling all units!" I shouted. "I have a visual on the ransom pickup team. They're moving into the Bluebell Island cluster in a boat, a very fast boat. That's on the *north* side of the peninsula, repeat, the *north* side."

A pilot's voice replied, "Okay, roger on that, Tango Sierra, we are on our way."

But the boat was already gone.

Four minutes later I stood astride my Bombardier Embrio, squinting into the halogen headlights of approaching cars. Overhead I could hear the whispering hiss of an FBI stealth helicopter.

One of the cars squealed to a halt next to me, and its doors flew open. First, three agents in dark suits jumped out. Then the driver emerged.

"Q.U.I.P.," I said quietly, "tag that car."

"Aye aye, Captain," said Q.U.I.P. in a Scottish brogue.

Silhouetted by the headlights behind her, Special Agent Dawson approached me, looming like an angry shadow. As she pointed at me, I saw the spark of a GPS tracer shoot from my Embrio past her to her car.

"Swift?" she hissed.

"Wait, don't tell me," I said. "Let me guess: They got away."

"Not yet," said Agent Dawson, turning toward the harbor. "We've spotted the boat floating near a dock on Farragut Island, just out—"

Her words were cut off by an explosion.

Behind the near island, a fireball rose like a flaming flower in the dark.

7

Bait and Switch

"No wonder they asked for thirty-five million," I said as Agent Dawson and her minions practically frog-marched me into the house. "If they keep blowing up their vehicles at this rate, they'll need another thirty-five pretty soon."

Sandy greeted us in the foyer.

"What happened?" she asked.

"It was a close call for the kidnappers," I said. "The FBI almost got within *miles* of them this time."

I nodded at Agent Dawson. Let's just say she was not amused.

But you can bet my cockiness melted quickly the moment I entered the living room and saw the pale look on my mom's face. She hurried up to me.

"You didn't see your father?" she asked. "Not at all?"

"No, I'm sorry, Mom," I said.

She dropped onto a chair, looking drained.

"What kind of game is this?" she said bitterly. "What is it they want?"

Special Agent Dawson took me hard by the arm. She gave my mom a no-nonsense look.

"Mrs. Swift," she said. "I'm sorry. I fully expect to see your husband released, perhaps even soon."

"Do you?" said Mom.

"Yes, but in the meantime, it's important that you keep your son under control," said Agent Dawson with a sharper tone. "I am *very* close to placing him in protective custody—for his own good and the good of the investigation. As it is, I'm now forced to assign an escort detail to him for the next seventy-two hours—a period of time I expect will be critical to the success of our operation."

"What operation would that be?" I asked, yanking my arm out of Dawson's grasp. "You mean the one where you give away our money and then get nothing in return?"

Now Dawson's eyes flashed angrily.

"You are confined to this house for the next seventy-two hours," she said huskily.

"You can't do that," I said.

"Please do *not* make me get a court order," she growled. "If I have to do that, I may get angry enough to file obstruction of justice charges." Her tight, controlled way of speaking was breaking down a bit. She turned sharply to a cohort of six agents waiting nearby. "Agents Bogenn and Bartley, I want a twenty-four-hour watch on young Mr. Swift here." Then Agent Dawson briskly crossed the room into the foyer, heels clicking on the marble floor. "The rest of you come with me immediately. Let's get gone."

I was so angry, I wanted to pick up the nearby flower vase and toss it at her exiting figure.

But as I watched her storm out of the house, I suddenly felt a hand on my arm.

I turned to see Sandy staring at me.

Her eyes were wide with surprise—and knowledge.

Twenty minutes later Sandy sat me at a workstation in her lab, just below mine in the bunker behind the house. Agents Bogenn and Bartley followed us down the translucent tunnels from the house to our lab complex. Once we entered Sandy's lab, they posted themselves outside the door.

"Okay, so what's got you so amped up?" I asked. Sandy often got excited about things, but right now she seemed ready to explode.

"Hey, Q.U.I.P.," she called. "You there?"

"I'm always here," answered Q.U.I.P. sullenly.

"You doing your job?" asked Sandy.

"What job?"

"Recording conversations."

"Oh, that job," said Q.U.I.P. "Yes."

"Can you play back the very last one?" asked Sandy. "I want the very last comments from Special Agent Francina Dawson as she walked out the door."

Q.U.I.P. made a sound like an old-fashioned audiotape scrolling backward, which, of course, was his idea of a joke, since he recorded digitally. Then he played back the requested snippet.

"Agents Bogenn and Bartley, I want a twenty-four-hour watch on young Mr. Swift here." The sound of heels clicking on a marble floor. *"The rest of you come with me immediately. Let's get gone."*

"That's it," said Sandy. "Now upload it into my computer, please."

"Would you like fries with that?" asked Q.U.I.P.

Sandy gave my wrist unit a look. "Sure," she said. "And please name the file 'Dawson dot zero one.'"

"Done," said Q.U.I.P.

Now Sandy plopped down on her chair at the keyboard and started tapping and clicking away with the mouse. First she played back the Dawson quotes to verify the upload. Then she pulled up the file through a program called Spectro-ID and played it back again. The program produced a "digital picture" of Dawson's voice in graphs that measured various components of its sound—pitch, tone, cadence, harmonic level, and so forth.

Finally she turned to me.

"Tom, come on," she said. "You heard it, didn't you?"

I was perplexed. "Heard what?"

She shook her head. "I guess you didn't because you were too angry at old Dawson. You let her get to you and forgot Dad's rule of observation."

Always observe things carefully. He said it all the time. *Especially when you're excited.*

"Okay," I nodded. "So what did you hear?"

Sandy highlighted and replayed a snippet of

Agent Dawson's speech: *"Let's get gone."*

"Tom, who else said that recently?" asked Sandy.

I thought for but a second; it came to me fast. "The lead kidnapper."

"Right," said Sandy. "The woman."

"But that woman had a very heavy Southern accent," I said. "Agent Dawson doesn't."

Sandy nodded. "Okay, now observe the power of voice analysis software." She pulled in another sound clip. "This is the kidnapper saying the same thing. I cleaned it up, knocking out all the background noise."

"Let's get gone!" said the recording in its deep Southern drawl. My eyes widened. Something about it . . . a quality of the anger . . . struck me as familiar.

Meanwhile the software program automatically created a digital sound picture with graphs.

"Now let's cross-analyze," said Sandy.

She clicked on the spectrographic breakdown of the kidnapper's voice and dragged it over the combined graphs of Agent Dawson's voice. The computer's hard drive whirred and clicked a few seconds. Then it emitted a pleasant bell tone. An analysis appeared in a results box:

VOICE MATCH CONFIRMED!
98.7 PERCENT PROBABILITY

Sandy and I stared at it.

"Holy crab cakes," I said.

It wasn't easy trying to act casual as we climbed the staircase from Sandy's lab up to my lab with Agents Bogenn and Bartley right behind us. Naturally, I wanted to spin to face them and yell, "Your boss is a totally demented wack-job!" But for all I knew, Bogenn and Bartley were in on the deal.

In my lab I popped up a satellite map of the Shopton area and said, "Okay, Q.U.I.P., give me the GPS overlay."

"What's this?" asked Sandy.

"I tagged Dawson's car with a tracking bug out by the harbor," I said. "At the time I wasn't sure why I had the overwhelming urge to do so. Apparently it was my infallible scum-detection instinct."

Sandy got a kick out of that. On the map a red dot started flashing. I clicked a few times to enlarge the area. The dot (which marked the location of the GPS bug on Agent Dawson's car) was moving through the Theodore Roosevelt State Park.

"What's she doing there?" asked Sandy. She glanced at her watch. "It's almost one thirty a.m."

I shook my head. "Look, she's heading up that old mining road toward the Motherlode." The Harrison Motherlode, an old silver-mining complex, had been abandoned for over a hundred years.

"Nobody goes up there," said Sandy.

We watched the red dot slow down and finally stop. I clicked to zoom in on the map and leaned closer to look. "'Number Seven Shaft,'" I read. I looked at Sandy. "We need to check it out . . . like, tomorrow morning." I glanced over at the lab door. "Without an FBI escort."

I printed out a copy of the map.

Then Sandy and I tried to brainstorm some ideas, but by two a.m. we were shot. We decided to get some sleep and powwow again in the morning.

The next morning I burst awake from a crazy dream in which I was an ant crawling through endless tunnels in a massive ant colony. As I woke, the great colony queen was waving her gigantic antennae in an awesome display of rage; every ant eye was on her. I sat up in bed grinning, then quickly grabbed a small notebook and started jotting notes.

Half an hour later I hustled down the hall to Sandy's room. I woke her and handed her a note.

"Give this to Mom," I said. "I'll wait here."

Sandy sat up and read over the note. Then a grin spread across her face.

"This should be fun," she said.

"Be sure to say hi to Agents Bartley and Bogenn for me, will you?"

"Oh, I most certainly will," said Sandy.

Then I flipped open my cell phone and called Andy Foger.

Twenty minutes later I left Sandy's room and went downstairs.

"Hi, guys," I said to my FBI escorts. "How's it going?"

They sat in chairs by the staircase. "It really couldn't be better," said Agent Bogenn, the taller one. He was reading a newspaper.

"Excellent," I said. "Say, I'm heading to the pantry for a little snack. Care to join me?"

"It would be our pleasure," said Agent Bartley, adjusting his glasses.

As we trudged down the front hall, I looked from agent to agent. "Do you guys like the FBI?" I asked.

"It's a great job," said Bogenn.

"A dream job, really," said Bartley.

I nodded. "It seems like it would be. But do you like your boss?"

The two agents exchanged a look.

"Special Agent Dawson is a fine supervisor," said Agent Bartley carefully.

We walked a few more steps in silence. Then Agent Bogenn added, "If you like your springs wound extra tight."

The two men started cracking up.

I grinned. "She does seem a little . . . high-strung sometimes," I said.

We entered the kitchen. Suddenly I heard my mother shouting in the living room—a rare sound in our house. "That's just not acceptable!" she yelled. "That's not good enough!" And then I head a shattering of glass.

Bogenn and Bartley glanced at each other, then looked at me. I frowned and shrugged.

We hurried into the living room. There, my mother

stood with a cordless phone in her hand. A red glass vase was shattered on the wood floor. She gave the two FBI agents a savage look and pointed at them.

"Where is Special Agent Dawson?" she said loudly.

The agents both looked rattled. "Are you receiving a contact call?" whispered Agent Bogenn. "Is that a perpetrator contact?"

Mom looked confused. "What are you talking about?" she asked. "I want Agent Dawson!"

I slowly stepped backward into the kitchen, then ducked behind the china cabinet. Moments later I heard Agent Bartley say, "Hey, where's Tom?"

"He's going out with Sandy!" shouted my Mom.

"Where?" I heard the men running across the room.

"Bartley, they're making a break for the garage!"

"Let's go!"

I heard their shoes thump across the marble foyer and out the front door. I stepped from my hiding place and peeked out the kitchen window just in time to see Sandy and a boy in my favorite baseball cap pulled low over his eyes in the Swift Speedster. The boy was driving; they peeled out of the driveway and veered onto the main road.

Seconds later Agents Bartley and Bogenn dived into their black sedan and immediately gave chase. As they pulled onto the main road too, I left the window and went into the living room, where Mom was sweeping up the broken red glass of the vase.

"Well done, Mom," I said with a smile.

"I was so confusing I even confused myself," she said.

"It certainly got their attention."

She frowned. "Are you sure you need to go investigate?"

"Oh, I'm sure," I said.

I went to the front closet where I'd hung my Chameleon Suit last night after the money drop-off and pickup. I draped it over me, then went outside and hopped aboard my Bombardier Embrio.

Five minutes later I pulled into a parking lot on the north side of town. The Speedster—which had morphed into a different shape and color—sat idling in one of the slots. Sandy sat in the passenger seat. Driving—and wearing my favorite baseball cap—was Andy Foger.

I pulled up next to the car.

"It troubles me that the FBI mistook you for me," I said to him.

"Well, that goes double for me."

"Why?" asked Sandy.

"Because he's ugly and I'm not," said Andy, pointing at me.

I grinned and stepped off my Embrio. "Here, Sandy, you take the gyrobike back and hang with Mom, okay?" I said. "We don't want her alone right now."

"Got it," said Sandy, hopping out of the Speedster.

"Slide over, hot dog," I said to Andy.

"Whatever," he said. "My car is better."

"Yeah, but I'm taller than you," I said.

"My family's richer."

"Okay, you win," I said.

I got behind the wheel. Our ultimate destination was the Harrison Motherlode mining complex. But first I had a quick detour planned. If Agent Dawson was indeed the lead kidnapper and her gang was hiding in an abandoned mine shaft, then a certain prototype vehicle might come in handy. So we made a quick stop at Swift Enterprises, where Dr. Victor Rashid already had the two-man

Mini-Worm mounted on a trailer for me.

We latched it onto the trailer hitch of the powerful Speedster and then hauled it up into the hills . . . where silver veins once ran underground.

8

A Boring Expedition

The high country outside Shopton was beautiful in the early summer morning. As we cruised up the old mining roads, I had Q.U.I.P. keep a sharp eye on Agent Dawson's location by monitoring the GPS bug planted on her car. It was still parked near the entrance of Number Seven Shaft.

After about ten minutes of switchback driving, I pulled over and checked the map.

"Okay, the next fork leads up to the Motherlode area," I said. "No doubt they have sentries posted. We'd better scout on foot."

Andy and I hopped out and moved quietly up the side of the road, keeping to the trees. It was heavily wooded here, so I got an idea.

"You stay here," I said to Andy.

"Why?"

I pushed the controller I held in my hand, activating the Chameleon Suit. "Because," I said.

Andy was stunned. "I . . . can't see you."

"Stay here," I repeated.

I moved up along the road, stepping carefully to avoid snapping twigs. As I rounded a bend, I could see the top of an old wooden structure. I snuck up a small slope and found myself looking down on the entrance to Number Seven Shaft, the largest shaft in the Motherlode complex. Narrow-gauge tracks for ore carts, overgrown with weeds, ran out of the entry building. Agent Dawson's car was parked near an old pump jack.

Nearby, three men in camouflage pants and T-shirts guarded the mine entrance. One held a rifle.

So much for the front door, I thought.

I surveyed the landscape around the mine approach. From the hillcrest, I could see a small side road curving up through the trees and around the hillock, where an entry tower rose. It looked like the perfect place for a wormhole. I quickly backtracked to Andy to report.

I said, "Dude, we'll have to drill our own side shaft."

Andy's eyes got big. "Really?"

"You don't look on board with this plan," I said.

Andy glanced nervously at the Mini-Worm. "That's because I don't trust your junky Swift technology."

I nodded. "Okay," I said. "Then just help me get it to a good starting spot."

"You're nuts, Swift."

"I want my dad back," I said. "If he's down there, I'm getting him out—and getting *your* dad off the hook too, by the way."

Andy knew I was right, so he didn't complain when we found the side road I'd spotted, drove slowly and quietly up to the hillside, then rolled the nine-hundred-pound Mini-Worm down the trailer ramp. It had small, retractable caterpillar tracks on the bottom, like a small tank or bulldozer, so the digger could travel over the uneven terrain.

I'd gotten a quick driving lesson from Victor back at Swift labs, so I unlatched the airtight canopy and lowered myself into the two-man cockpit.

"Last chance, Andy," I said.

"No way," he replied. "Besides, what if you *do* find your old man down there? You want an empty seat for him."

I blinked. "Wow. Good point. I'm an idiot not to have thought of that."

Andy just stared at me, then shook his head.

I fastened the shoulder-harness mechanism. I knew I'd be tilted or even inverted at times during the drilling, so I tightened the harness buckle. "Hey, if I don't come out alive, be sure to help Sandy turn the evidence on Dawson," I said.

Andy nodded.

"See you," I said. I pushed the starter button and the Worm jumped to life, humming low. I flicked on the cockpit controls and pulled the titanium canopy shut with a hissing thunk. Soft interior lights flickered on, and I could hear the light breath of the oxygen system.

I had approximately four hours of air. I could see out a pair of polycarbonate-acrylic alloy windows, each clear as glass but tougher than steel.

I waved to Andy. He waved back.

"Here I come, Dad," I said.

I slid the caterpillar-track shifter into forward gear and nudged the control stick a bit. The Mini-Worm started rolling forward. Halfway up the slope I twisted a console dial. Through the forward window

I could see the nose-cone driller start to rotate.

Then I jammed the stick all the way forward.

Hydraulic lifts raised the Mini-Worm's back end, tilting her nose down. I could feel almost no vibration as the big drill bit sliced easily into the dirt. Within seconds the vehicle's nose was buried in the ground. As it dug deeper, I could hear the caterpillar tracks slowly retract into the fuselage of the Mini-Worm. Soon, I knew, the unit would be as round and smooth as a bullet.

Amazing! I thought. It was a gorgeous, elegant invention.

Now it was time to rescue its inventor.

Thirty minutes later I chewed through a rock wall into a dark, dingy tunnel. As I emerged, I quickly extended the caterpillar tracks again.

"Shaft Delta Four, I believe," said Q.U.I.P.

"Which way now, navigator?" I asked.

"Hang a right and look for the Pump 'N' Go," said Q.U.I.P. "We can gas up and ask for directions."

I laughed.

I admit I've been an impulsive risk taker on occasion. But I'm not stupid, nor am I suicidal. I wasn't just digging blindly. The night before, I'd found an amazing 3-D surveyor's map of the entire Harrison Motherlode mine complex. Mine maps are notoriously inaccurate, but this one was created recently using a "groundhog robot" exploration system with laser range finders. The new technology was producing remarkably accurate 3-D maps of old, abandoned mines.

"Q.U.I.P., how we doing?" I asked. Q.U.I.P. was using GPS software to monitor our position.

"I've got us linked to the Motherlode-range scan data," said Q.U.I.P. "Care for a mint?"

"No thanks," I said.

"Continue forward another twenty meters, then bore into the left wall," said Q.U.I.P. "Once you get the nose in, I'll get you oriented again."

Telemetry gathered from the robots in the mapping expedition had produced some interesting data about the Motherlode complex. Q.U.I.P.'s analysis had pinpointed the most likely place where the kidnappers might be hiding comfortably. A large room, built for equipment storage, sat about eight hundred meters down Number Seven Shaft. The room, called "The Hotel" by silver miners a century ago, had two big intake air shafts that kept it well ventilated. Several small side tunnels converged there as well.

Soon I had the caterpillar tracks retracted again and the Mini-Worm was digging once more.

"Do you think they can hear us coming?" I asked Q.U.I.P.

"Possibly. But my sensors indicate a 97.9 percent chance that auxiliary air pumps are running 24-7, making it difficult to hear our approach—that is, until we pop out into the shaft, scaring the bejabbers out of everyone."

The plan, of course, was to aim for one of the side shafts, which were most likely deserted. Sure enough, about twenty minutes later the Mini-Worm nosed out into another dark tunnel, in a spot just fifty yards uphill from The Hotel.

The noise of our emergence was probably pretty loud—so loud that the kidnappers, fearing a cave in, might not investigate. Just in case, I strapped a minibreather over my nose and mouth, popped open the hatch, and activated my Chameleon Suit. As I climbed out of the cockpit, I lifted the breather a bit to test the mine air. It was thin and musty, but quite breathable. I removed the breather to save the oxygen in case I needed it later.

I quietly asked, "Which way?"

"Left," whispered Q.U.I.P.

Using an infrared headlamp and my special visor again, I had good, well-lit vision without fear of detection as I moved down the tunnel. And I wasn't worried about getting lost, because I knew Q.U.I.P. was mapping my progress and marking the Mini-Worm's location.

Suddenly I heard voices echoing down the dark, dank corridor.

"Do you hear that, Q.U.I.P.?" I asked.

"Yes," he said.

"Can you make out what they're saying?"

"I'm filtering it now." Q.U.I.P. paused a second. "Yes, their commentary suggests that they heard us arrive. I detect anxiety. I believe they're withdrawing deeper into the mine."

Sure enough, the voices quickly receded, as if moving away.

"Q.U.I.P.?"

"Yes, boss?"

"Be sure to let me know if you hear Dad's voice."

"Of course," replied Q.U.I.P.

"Thanks."

Q.U.I.P. beeped. "I'm a computer," he said. "Don't thank me." He whirred and clicked: his idea of a joke. "By the way, I detect light up ahead."

I flipped up my visor—yep, light. I moved farther along the tunnel.

I crept around a curve—and gasped.

I stood at the opening to what had to be The Hotel, a large circular room at least a hundred feet in diameter. It had been transformed into fairly cozy living quarters, with soft-looking beanbag chairs, dozens of plants, banks of full-spectrum lights, and several large coolers. One cooler near me was open and filled with soft drinks, blocks of cheese, and a plastic bag filled with shiny red apples.

"The Hotel, *indeed*," commented Q.U.I.P.

But the most amazing thing was a large sausage-shaped vehicle sitting on a platform near the far wall of the room. Like the Mini-Worm, its tapered nose had the sharp steely glint of a polished, unused drill bit. But this drilling machine was at least as big as the Mega-Worm back in the Swift lab—perhaps even bigger.

"Good gosh," I said. "It's massive."

"No wonder they needed thirty-five million bucks," said Q.U.I.P.

I looked around: Nobody in sight. I crossed the room to take a closer look at the borer. Then I noticed its name embossed on the side: *Mole One*. I frowned. Was this really the Foger Utility Group vehicle? If so, was Randall Foger the mastermind behind Dad's kidnapping after all? That would certainly put a twist in the unfolding plot.

Just for fun, I pulled out another magnetic GPS tag and stuck it on the digger's aft side.

"Good thinking," said Q.U.I.P.

"You never know," I replied.

As I walked around the huge machine looking for more clues or markings, I found a smaller room cut into the rock on the far side. It was obviously some sort of control room; a long workstation ran the length of the wall. A bank of monitors glowed above a console filled with lit, multicolored buttons and digital readouts.

Everything looked recently assembled, brand-new. But someone had used red paint to splash a messy-looking message across the front panels of the workstation.

It read: FIGHT FIRE WITH FIRE!

"What the heck does *that* mean?" I asked. "What 'fire' are they fighting?"

"Hey, who's there?" shouted a voice from one of the side corridors.

I froze as footsteps approached.

"Someone's in the command pod!" shouted another voice.

The Worm Turns

I looked down. Against the complicated background of the computer console, the Chameleon Suit wasn't working so well. Three men, all with long hair and beards, rushed into The Hotel from another side tunnel.

The lead one halted, looking strangely at me.

"What is it?" he said.

The two other men stepped up beside him. They also had odd looks on their faces. I realized that, although visible, I probably looked more like a flickering phantom than a person with a cape. Their hesitation gave me the moment I needed to figure out a response.

I reached into a pouch I wore on my hip and grabbed one of the strobe grenades I'd packed last night for the trip. I pulled its activation switch and tossed it out in front of me, where it detonated with a loud pop less than a second later.

The dazzling, repetitive flashing blinded the men. I was prepared, of course—I wore special contact lenses designed to neutralize the strobe effect. I knew the grenade lasted only about fifteen seconds, so I turned and ran down the darkest looking side shaft. Soon the shouting receded behind me, and I turned into a wider tunnel, knowing I was essentially invisible again.

Invisible, perhaps—but not alone. Once again I heard quiet voices up ahead. I plugged an earbud into my wrist unit so Q.U.I.P. could speak directly into my ear without being heard. Then I whispered, "What's up ahead?"

Q.U.I.P. didn't answer right away. After a few seconds he said, "One person is asking questions. They sound very technical, boss. Something about a gyroscopic guidance system and . . . wait. Wait. The other voice is a woman's. I'm running the voice ID and, yes, son of a gun, it's Agent Dawson."

"Agent Dawson is up ahead?" I whispered.

"Correct," said Q.U.I.P. "She's . . . *quietly agitated*, is

"What is it about bad guys and leg shackles?" I asked as I inserted the pick into the lock. "Don't they know how useless they are?" Within seconds the lock clicked open, and I pulled apart the shackle.

Dad reached down and rubbed his ankle for a few seconds.

"Ah, much better," he said.

"Dad, who are these people?"

He looked up at me, surprised. "Don't you know?"

"Well, the FBI is calling it a case of industrial espionage on steroids," I said. "They think Randall Foger and FUG are behind it."

"Randall Foger? They really think that?" He shook his head, incredulous. "No, Tom, this is a TRB operation all the way."

"TRB? But then . . . why is FUG's tunnel-digging mole sitting just down the hall?"

"I don't know," he said. "It just arrived yesterday. I'm pretty sure they stole it. How, I don't know." He stood up. "The woman asked me a number of questions about calibration and so forth. I believe they plan to use it for something big today—but I don't know what."

"Dad, that woman," I said. "She's an FBI agent."

Dad gaped. "What?"

I nodded. "In fact, she's the lead agent on your kidnapping case."

"Unbelievable," said Dad. He was clearly shaken. "They told me she's a new TRB convert, yet she's calling all the shots here. I guess I know why now."

"According to Andy Foger, the FBI's got the FUG labs all locked down and evacuated," I said. "That's probably how she got access to the Mole One."

I heard some rustling down the opposite shaft. "Better get going," I said. "Can you walk?"

Dad stood up. "I'm fine."

I led him back the way I'd come. It wasn't far to the main room. But as we approached, we could hear a lot of commotion, including the rumbling of a large engine.

"Wait here," I said to Dad.

Checking to make sure my Chameleon Suit was activated, I moved slowly to the room opening and slid along the wall. There I saw several men preparing to close the main hatch of the Mole One.

Inside, Francina Dawson barked out orders. Her Southern accent was as thick as molasses.

"Ya'll make sure that trailer is hitched right," she said with irritation. "You people and your technology phobias will be the *death* of me, I swear."

Then she pulled the hatch shut. A few seconds later the Mole One rumbled off its platform on caterpillar tracks similar to those of the Mini-Worm. The massive machine rolled slowly across the room and up the main exit shaft. The small platoon of men followed, leaving The Hotel completely deserted.

I hustled back to Dad.

"They're moving the Mole," I said.

"Did they say where?"

"No," I said. I grinned. "But we'll know soon enough."

"How?"

"Trust me."

Dad grinned back. "I always trust you, son."

Fifteen minutes later Dad was my copilot in the Mini-Worm as it tracked back through the tunnel we'd bored into Number Seven Shaft. Since we were crawling through a previously drilled route, passage was swift.

"At this rate, we'll be out in another five minutes," I said. "This is a sweet machine, Dad."

"Thanks." He gave me a fatherly look. "And thanks for coming after me."

I grinned. "It was a no-brainer decision."

"How are your mother and sister holding up?" he asked.

"They're okay. You can imagine, though. Mom was on the edge, but she hung in there for us, you know."

"Of course," said Dad. "She's amazing."

I adjusted the pitch of the nose slightly. "Sandy and I considered the possibility that it was really TRB behind the kidnapping," I said. "But when they didn't make their usual boastful claim of responsibility, I was confused."

Dad nodded. "Yes, The Road Back always makes a big PR show out of every radical stunt they pull."

"So why didn't they this time?"

Dad shrugged. "Clearly they have something else planned and don't want to blow their cover," he said. "Say, can we get word out yet?"

"Not this deep underground," I said. "I have Q.U.I.P. trying, though. When he makes cellular contact, I'll put you on my phone—right to Mom, I hope."

Then, as if on cue, I saw a glimmer of light up ahead. In minutes the Mini-Worm's nose jutted up into the air, showing nothing but blue summer sky above us through the acrylic front window. And then my cell phone rang.

I looked at the number and flipped it open. "Andy, what's up?" I said, then added: "Hey, I got my dad back!"

"Swift, the goons left the mine, all of them," said Andy Foger, sounding distressed. "And they have my dad's driller! They drove into a huge honking truck." There was a pause, and then he added, "I think they're heading back toward Shopton with it. Are they whacked or what? Dude, I'm watching them drive down the hill toward town right now."

"Andy, where are you?" I asked.

"Just down that side road from where I dropped you off."

"Well, drive back up," I said. "We're out of the mines. Let's get the Worm on the trailer." I hesitated, but then I thought I'd better spill the beans, since Andy's family was so deeply involved too. "Listen, I think Dawson's planning to use your Mole for something nasty."

"Great," he said. "And we'll get blamed."

"No way," I said. "It's TRB. They're behind the whole thing, with that Dawson woman on their payroll, working the inside at the FBI."

"Okay, I can see you now," said Andy, and hung up.

Sure enough, the Speedster swung around just below us as the Mini-Worm bounced down the hill. It was kind of weird to see a Foger driving a Swift-designed vehicle. Andy backed the trailer to the edge of the road, then hopped out. But he couldn't get its ramp manually extended. I waited a few minutes, then finally popped open the canopy to help. But the ramp was stuck in its slot.

"Great," I said.

It took us another five minutes of yanking to get it out. Then I hopped back into the Mini-Worm and steered it up the ramp onto the trailer. The three of us strapped it down and hopped into the car.

"I've got Mrs. Swift on the line," said Q.U.I.P. suddenly.

I smiled, flipped opened my cell phone, and handed it to Dad.

"Mary?" he said.

I heard my mom's voice gush with happiness and relief in his ear. Dad assured her he was okay.

"We're coming home right now," he said.

As they talked a bit more, he quickly explained the situation and warned her about Agent Dawson's betrayal. He listened a moment, nodding. He looked over at me and said, "Your mom says they've already got a new lead investigator on the case. And I'm supposed to tell you she's working with Harlan Ames."

"Ha!" I said. "Good."

Then my wrist unit buzzed. I looked down.

"Excuse me," said Q.U.I.P. "I'm monitoring the GPS tag you placed on Mole One."

"Yeah?" I said. In the excitement of finding Dad, I'd forgotten about it. "Where'd they take it?"

"Skylark Hollow," said Q.U.I.P.

I gripped the steering wheel. "Are you sure?"

"Yes."

"Dad!" I called.

He was just saying good-bye to Mom. He flipped the phone shut and said, "What is it, Tom?"

I pointed at the phone and said, "I think you need to call Harlan *immediately*."

"Why?"

"According to our readings, TRB just hauled the Mole One to Skylark Hollow."

Dad gave me a look. "That's at the base of the hill behind Swift Tower."

"Exactly," I said. "Dad, I think we've got about thirty minutes to evacuate our building!"

Dad started punching numbers. I turned to Andy.

"Dude, dial 9-1-1," I said.

Mole Hole

I'd never before driven the Speedster at high speed down mountain roads with a thousand-pound trailer load hitched to the back. So after a couple of dangerous, near-jackknifing turns, I slowed down until I reached the smooth county highway leading back to Shopton.

"Pedal to the metal, dude!" cried Andy from the backseat.

I glanced over at Dad.

He nodded. "Go for it, son."

"We'll have a police escort shortly," called Andy. "I just talked to Captain Davis. He's sending out cruisers to link up with us."

"Did you send them to Skylark Hollow, too?" I called.

"Of course!" shouted Andy over the engine whine. "Do you think I'm an idiot?"

I glanced back at him. "Should I really answer that?"

Andy guffawed. His laugh sounded like a cross between a dying donkey and a stadium horn. He leaned forward from the backseat.

"You know, I didn't think you'd help me clear my dad's name," he said. "So I guess I owe you something." He paused. "A cookie, maybe."

"Maybe," I said.

I kicked in the accelerator as we pulled onto the county highway.

The Swift Tower was on the opposite end of town, but I knew a way to bypass the downtown area and avoid city traffic. Skylark Hollow was an unincorporated, mostly undeveloped neighborhood next to the Shopton municipal golf course. It was a beautiful area, very woody and secluded, full of trails and culs-de-sac and an occasional mansion rising out of the trees.

"There's our escort!" called Dad, pointing up ahead.

Two Shopton Police cruisers, lights flashing, sat

one on either side of the road. As we whizzed past, they fell in behind us.

Q.U.I.P. buzzed and beeped. I glanced at my wrist. Numbers were scrolling up the display screen.

"Quit acting like a computer," I said.

"Can't help it," said Q.U.I.P. "It's fun."

"Do you have something for us?"

Q.U.I.P. sniffed. "Maybe," he said. "Okay, yes. I've been monitoring the police band, and it appears they found the TRB caravan of vehicles on a hillside near Harvest House Inn. After surrounding the area, they moved in and apprehended eleven suspects—all white males, some armed, but no resistance offered."

"All white males?" I repeated.

"Unfortunately, yes," reported Q.U.I.P. "And the Mole One transport trailer was empty. Officers are currently following the tracks."

As I approached a red light at an intersection, one of the police cruisers suddenly sped ahead of us, siren blaring. It pulled carefully into the intersection, blocking cross traffic. The officer at the wheel thrust out his arm and waved us on through.

"Awesome," said Andy.

I waved at the officer as we sped through the intersection.

"And here's an update," said Q.U.I.P. "Officers on the scene now report that a double-tracked trail leads up the hillside behind Swift Tower—and disappears into a large, cavelike hole that looks, and I quote, 'recently excavated.'"

"Yeah, like five minutes ago," I said grimly. "No doubt Dawson is in the Mole, and she's headed for the tower." I looked over at Dad. "Could she cause a catastrophic collapse?"

Dad shook his head. "It would be very difficult for her to bring it down unless she knew exactly which support structures to hit," he said. "As you know, Swift Tower was built to withstand hurricanes. But I have no doubt that a five-thousand-pound machine with a one-ton drill bit can cause a lot of damage."

"Try *eight* thousand pounds," said Andy proudly.

I nodded. "Thanks, Andy," I said dryly.

"Hey, a scientist needs all the facts," he replied.

My phone rang again. Dad answered.

"Hey, Harlan," he said. "Okay, good. Thanks. We're almost there. Is Victor nearby? Let me talk to him." He chatted briefly with Victor Rashid, asking him about some equipment. Then he got back on with Harlan. "Help Victor put a team together ASAP, okay? Thanks, Harlan. Yeah, I feel good. I'll see you in a minute." He hung up.

"The tower's evacuated, right?" I asked hopefully.

Dad nodded with a relieved sigh.

"So how can we stop this maniac?" asked Andy. "Follow her down the hole in your Mini-Worm?"

Up ahead I caught the first glimpse of the thirty-story structure, gleaming against the dark, wooded hill behind it. I knew there wouldn't be time to get behind the hill and catch the Mole before it drilled into the tower.

"I think we'll have to cut her off at the pass, so to speak," said Dad.

"But how can we locate her if she's coming under the hill?" I asked.

"I've got Victor putting out a team with some GPR equipment we've been developing for utility companies," he replied. "We'll also plug a cable into the media pod of the Mini-Worm."

"What's GPR?" I asked.

"Ground-penetrating radar," replied Dad. "Our units can detect even small plastic pipes and cables, so an eight-thousand-pound, metallic mole-monster should be easy to find."

I swerved around some road construction signs, feeling the heavy trailer swaying behind the Speedster.

"And you say the Worm has a media pod?" I asked.

"Yes," said Dad. "Since drillers tend to lose radio contact when underground, we developed a heavy-duty com-link cable that attaches to an aft pod on the Worm. They'll feed it in behind us as we drill, and we can keep in touch as the GPR locators get readings on the Mole's movement."

"Awesome!" I said. "We can cut her off!"

"Yes," said Dad. "Although I'm not exactly sure what we can do once Worm meets Mole."

"You'll be outweighed ten to one," said Andy.

Dad turned to him. "Are you familiar with the specs for the Mole?" he asked.

"A little."

"Is there a weak spot we can exploit?" he asked. "A critical power or control casing, something external we can aim for?"

Andy looked reluctant. I guess I couldn't blame

him. After all, we were talking about ramming his dad's gazillion-dollar baby. But good sense overcame his resistance quickly. Once again I had to acknowledge that maybe Andy wasn't such a self-centered, blowhard scum-bucket after all.

"Well," he said, "the drive assembly computers are directly behind the nose, up on top. In a small, humped compartment for easy access. Tucked right behind the back rim of the drill bit."

"Wow," I said as I pulled into the Swift Tower parking lot. "Tough target."

"Hey, if you even *find* the Mole underground, I'll be amazed," said Andy.

I swung the Speedster around to the back parking lot, at the base of the hill. Victor, Harlan, and a team of technicians were already fanning out up the hillside, pushing wheeled GPR units that looked like big lawn mowers. Each unit had a radar screen mounted between the push handles.

Sandy was there too. She came sprinting up and dived into Dad's arms.

"How's it going, Madame Curie?" he asked, hugging her tightly.

"Good, Daddy," she said. She pulled back and looked up at his face. "You look tired."

Dad smiled. "I am, but there's no time for sleep. We have a tower to save."

Andy and I already had the ramp extended from the trailer, and I scrambled up into the Mini-Worm's cockpit. Then I backed it down and turned its nose uphill. Dad gave Sandy a quick squeeze and turned to wave at an approaching group of people.

"Hello, folks," he called.

One of them, a handsome, dark-skinned young man hauling a big spool of com-link cable, smiled a dazzling smile. "Dr. Swift, it is so good to see you," he cried.

"Let's get plugged in quickly, Ranjeet," said Dad.

Ranjeet Patel was head of computers and information technology for Swift Enterprises. Only twenty-eight, he was incredibly good at his job and also one of the nicest guys I'd ever met. I loved his Indian accent straight from Bangalore, his home and the Silicon Valley of India.

I watched them plug and lock the cable into a small metal box on the back end of the Mini-Worm. Then

Ranjeet plugged the other end into a small, battery-powered communications console that resembled a laptop computer, with a keyboard and display screen. He adjusted a small microphone stand attached to the console.

"Hello, can you hear me?" he said into the mike.

Ranjeet's voice came out of a radio speaker on the Mini-Worm's control console.

"Loud and clear," I said.

Ranjeet smiled again as Dad crawled into the cockpit. "I hear you, too," he said.

"What do we do now?" I asked.

Ranjeet tapped a few keys on his console. "Look on your display screen," he said.

A small screen flickered to life on the Mini-Worm's console panel. I stared at the image displayed there.

"Looks like a topographical map," I said.

"Very good," said Panjeet. "This is indeed the hill behind the Swift Tower. The blue triangle on the screen is your Mini-Worm, and the blue number next to it is your depth—that is, your position relative to ground level. Now, we have all of the GPR units on a wireless network linked into this display. The moment any one of the units detects the Mole

One, the vehicle will appear on-screen as a red triangle with a red depth number."

"Brilliant, Ranjeet," said my Dad in admiration.

"This will help you find an intercept point," continued Ranjeet. "We also plotted that green line running down the center. It marks the most direct route from the coordinates of the Mole's hole to the Swift Tower. I would guess that the driller is following this route, or at least some approximation of it."

I thought, *Looks like I'm playing a video game with deadly stakes.*

I fired up the track motor and, using the console display, steered the Mini-Worm right atop the green line. Then I followed the line, heading uphill and away from the Swift Tower for about a hundred yards. I wanted a healthy margin of error in case Agent Dawson came at the tower from an unexpected angle. Finally, I turned the worm to face downhill, toward the tower. We wanted to hit the Mole's computer module from above and behind, if possible.

"What now?" I asked.

Dad patted my shoulder. "Now we wait," he said.

◇ ◇ ◇ ◇

Fifteen minutes later the parking lot was crawling with police and federal authorities. Swift workers who couldn't bear to go home stood outside a wide circle roped off around the perimeter of Swift Tower.

Captain Ron Davis, the tactical commander at the scene, stepped up to the open cockpit where Dad and I sat.

"We found a printed statement on one of the men in custody, written three months ago, according to the document date," he said. "Wanna hear it?"

"Sure," said Dad.

I nodded too, my hand tensely gripping the control stick.

Captain Davis read a rambling and typical TRB manifesto about inhumane technology, immoral science, et cetera, and calling for a complete halt to the dangerous activities taking place in Swift Enterprises, Foger Utility Group, and other similar dens of evil. It ended with the sentence, "When the Tower of Technology falls, let nothing but Pure Nature rise from the rubble!"

Dad shook his head. "When the Tower falls," he repeated. "So this was the plan all along."

"Chilling," said Davis.

Suddenly the console display beeped. I looked down to see a red triangle appear near the top of the map. The red depth indicator read "22 m." And according to the map scale, it was within four meters of the green line, so Panjeet's guess was almost right on the money.

"Here we go," I said.

Dad reached up and pulled shut the hatch as I flicked on the Air Supply switch. A small gauge lit up.

"Oxygen check," he said.

"Looks like we're good for almost three hours."

Dad looked grim. "This will be over long before then."

"I sure hope so," I said.

Panjeet's voice crackled in the console speakers. "The initial reading shows the Mole is traveling at approximately fifty-three meters per hour."

"Sweet!" I said. "Our rig goes faster than that." I was worried that the Mole might outrun us once it slipped past.

I jammed the control stick forward. The Mini-Worm tilted nose down and began to dig.

◇ ◇ ◇ ◇

Panjeet's topographical display was great. As we bur-
rowed downward, I kept referring to the on-screen
triangle markers and depth indicators to maintain an
intercept bearing. Dad helped me.

"We want to be at a shallow angle when we strike,"
he said. "Flatten out a bit."

Within fifteen minutes I was directly above the
Mole's projected path, with a slight downward tilt.
We stopped to wait at about eighteen meters deep.
Timing now was everything. If I went too soon, the
Mole would chew right through us, a pretty unpleas-
ant scenario. But if I went too late and we missed the
Mole, I'd have to slowly arc upward to take another
pass. By then it might be too late.

"Looks like T minus three minutes before Mole
passes the intercept," said Panjeet over the console.

"Ready to drill," I said.

"She's closing," said Panjeet.

Dad and I stared at the screen, watching the red
triangle approach. Seconds later we could feel the
first powerful hints of the violent churning. The
sheer force of the vibration grew and grew, and for
a second I felt panic. Were Panjeet's readings off?
Were we in the Mole's path, about to become human

confetti? It felt like it, and my hand trembled on the stick.

"She's almost right under you!" cried Panjeet.

Indeed the display showed that. But even Dad looked alarmed as the throbbing grew more intense. We exchanged a worried look.

"Should I pull back?" I asked.

"Maybe a bit," said Dad.

I didn't need a second permission. I yanked back on the stick, reversing the drill bit's rotation. The Mini-Worm slowly moved backward up the tunnel we'd bored. I stopped just ten meters or so farther back, even though we were shaking violently.

"It's passing beneath you!" shouted Panjeet. "It's . . . it's past your position!"

Looking down the short stretch of tunnel ahead, I saw no sign of the Mole. Panjeet had been right. It was below us all the time.

"Great," I said.

"Gun it, Tom!" said Dad quickly.

I shifted into forward, and the Mini-Worm jumped down the already drilled stretch of tunnel. Then we hit solid rock again. In just seconds we emerged into the large tube that the Mole had just drilled.

"We missed it!" I shouted.

Suddenly a new voice barked from the console speakers. It was a familiar one: Randall Foger!

"Tom, can you hear me?" he called.

I almost answered until I realized he was talking to my Dad, his ex-partner and now bitter rival.

"I hear you, Randall," said Dad. "What do you have for us?"

The Mini-Worm dropped into the Mole's tunnel with a thud. I quickly dropped the caterpillar tracks from their recessed compartments, then started following the newly bored passage. Within seconds I was right on the Mole One's tail. Acrylic-covered lamps cast a bright halogen glow on the backside of the big digger.

"You should see a pair of huge hydraulic cylinders housed on the Mole's back end," said Mr. Foger.

"See them?" said Dad, pointing. "Those big barrel-shaped things on the back."

I saw them all right. The Mole was pushing drilled rock and dirt back at us as it chewed ahead, but I caught good glimpses of its tail.

"Those power the drill mechanism," said Randall Foger.

"And so?" said my Dad.

"So ram them," said Mr. Foger.

Dad turned to look at me. "Well, you heard the man."

I smiled grimly. "Roger that," I said.

And I eased the stick forward.

Ranjeet's voice returned to the console, sounding alarmed. "The Mole is now seventy meters from the tower's foundation—and closing rapidly. She's increased speed to eighty meters per hour. Moving very fast. Not good."

But the Mole was digging through hard rock. We were merely slicing through loose debris, so within seconds we were right on its tail.

Randall Foger's voice came on again. "Tom, I should mention that the cylinders are highly pressurized, as you might expect," he said blandly.

"How highly?" asked Dad.

"*Highly*. So be careful."

"Hang on, Dad," I said. And I rammed the stick forward.

When I woke up, my head was ringing. And I was sitting in total, perfect darkness.

I felt around. The cockpit seemed intact. I reached over and put a hand on my dad, who wasn't moving. I quickly dug into my pouch, pulled out a miniflashlight, and shined it on Dad's face. He had a bloody gash, but it didn't look too deep. Then his eyes flickered open.

"Tom?" he said.

"Yeah, Dad." My head was pounding. "I think we both hit the console pretty hard."

"Did we stop the Mole?" he asked.

I shined the light out the front window, which was covered in a viscous fluid—engine oil, no doubt. The nose of the Mini-Worm was buried in one of the barrel-shaped cylinders of the Mole. Both of the cylinders had clearly ruptured, and oil was everywhere. Aside from a low hum, there was no sound. Suddenly tiny side lights flashed on in the cockpit. Then a red gauge lit up on the console.

A pleasant female voice said, "Emergency backup systems activated. Airflow resumed."

Dad and I both sighed at the same time.

"I love you, whoever you are," I called out to the voice.

Dad combined a chuckle with a pained groan.

"I don't think this vehicle is moving from here," he said. "My guess is that we are officially movement-disabled."

"How do we get back topside?"

"Walk," said Dad.

He reached into a small front compartment and pulled out two medium-size oxygen tanks. Each had shoulder straps and a tube running to a breathing mask.

"Cool," I said.

"We'll wear these just in case. Then we'll follow the com-link cable back up to the surface."

". . . Can you hear me?" crackled Panjeet's voice on the console. "Dr. Swift? Thomas?"

"Ah, we're back online," said Dad. "We hear you, Panjeet. We're alive, but we took quite a kick in the teeth."

"The Mole no longer moves," reported Panjeet.

"And neither does the Worm," I said. "So we're coming up on foot."

"Oh my goodness," said Panjeet.

Now Captain Davis came on. "We're coming in from up top," he said. "I have two officers with oxygen. They'll follow your cable."

"Okay," I said. "We'll meet them halfway. Out."

We unhitched our shoulder harnesses and wriggled into the straps for the oxygen tanks. Then we positioned our masks. Dad unlatched the canopy and we pushed hard. The Mole's tunnel was just barely high enough to let us squeeze out of the cockpit with the tanks on our backs.

Using my flashlight to see, we crawled over rock debris to the back of the Mini-Worm and each grabbed the com-link cable. Then we used it to pull ourselves along the tunnel. But suddenly something occurred to me.

"Dad?" I asked. "What about Agent Dawson?"

We both stopped.

"You're right, son," said Dad.

Without hesitation, we turned around. I led the way as we squeezed around the Mini-Worm. The explosion had blown the two cylinder barrels apart, rending a jagged hole in the back of the Mole One. I shined the flashlight inside, which revealed a rear storage compartment filled with shattered containers. With Dad's help I crawled up inside. The forward door was bent from the impact, but I managed to ram it open with my shoulder.

I stepped forward into a four-person cockpit. Only one person was in there, however: Francina Dawson, FBI agent, TRB contractor, and right now, unconscious woman suffering from the effects of oxygen deprivation.

She was on the floor, and I could see she was gasping.

I took in a deep breath and then held it as I whipped off my breathing mask and placed it over Agent Dawson's face. As she breathed in the oxygen, she stirred a bit, but her eyes didn't open.

"Dad!" I shouted. "She's alive, but there's no oxygen! I'm sharing my mask with her!"

"I'll relay the news to Captain Davis!" he shouted back. "We'll get another o-tank down here."

"And a stretcher!" I shouted with the last of my breath.

I took back the oxygen mask for a couple more deep breaths, then held it over Agent Dawson's face again. Suddenly I remembered my minibreather. I'd saved it back in the Motherlode because of the fresh-air shafts. I strapped the oxygen mask onto Dawson's face, dug the minibreather out of my side pouch, and put it on.

And I sat with Agent Dawson while Dad radioed up to the surface.

It didn't take long for the first two officers to reach us. Minutes later a second pair arrived with extra oxygen and a stretcher. Within half an hour I stood on the surface, watching paramedics load Francina Dawson into an ambulance.

Nearby, Dad stood talking with Captain Davis and Randall Foger.

"Both machines are in pretty bad shape," he said.

"I don't think my insurance will cover the loss of Mole One," said Mr. Foger. He gave my Dad a look. "Maybe I'll have to sue you for damages."

Dad gave him a wry smile. "My lawyers are better than your lawyers," he said.

"Probably," said Mr. Foger. "Andy?"

Andy walked up, gazing over at the Swift Speedster. "I really want a car like that," he said.

"Let's go invent one," said Mr. Foger. He nodded to my father and the police captain. "Gentlemen?"

"Good-bye, Randall," said my dad.

I gave Andy a half wave. "I guess we'll go back to being enemies again, huh?" I said.

Andy gave me his wolf grin. "Just keep out of my

way, Swift, and nothing bad will happen to you."

"Gotcha," I said.

And off went the Foger family, leaving their multimillion-dollar drill bit buried next to Swift Tower.

Welcome Back!

The next day Swift Enterprises threw one of the best parties I had ever had the pleasure to attend. It had everything: a crushed-ice mountain filled with succulent shrimp and bowls of spicy cocktail sauce; a tropical-punch fountain splashing into a glowing pool covered by dry-ice fog; huge mounds of ham, roast beef, turkey, and every kind of cheese imaginable; and tons of other food and drink.

And that was just in the main conference room.

People milled around, laughing and shaking hands and hugging. Something about a near catastrophe got people thinking about what they might miss if, say, the whole Swift Tower had tumbled. A big "Welcome Back!" sign hung across the main lobby, and Dad's favorite local jazz band played on a stage nearby.

Harlan Ames walked up to me as I stood alone, looking around at the faces I knew so well.

"Tom, I owe you a lot," he said, wrapping his big, meaty hand around the back of my neck and giving a gentle squeeze.

"Why?" I said.

"You didn't give up. You believed in me."

I gave him a mystified look. "We all believed in you," I said. "I mean, why wouldn't we? You're . . . you're Harlan Ames." I shook my head and grinned. "If I can't count on Harlan Ames, I might as well just give up."

He expelled his famous gruff laugh.

"I appreciate what you did, regardless," he said.

I gazed across the room and noticed Casmir Trent sitting on the edge of a chair. Amazingly, despite the broken ribs and collarbone, he had insisted on being here. One arm was wrapped up tight and tucked into a sling. He held a small plate of shrimp in this hand while drinking a soda with the other.

"Let's give that man a hand," I said to Harlan.

We crossed the room and I snatched the plate from Casmir's hand. "Mister, put that shrimp down," I said.

Harlan clucked his tongue. "You know better, Casmir," he said. "The doctor said no weight bearing with that arm for at least a week."

Casmir gave him a sardonic look. "I can handle a shrimp."

Harlan leaned over to examine the plate. "But that's a *jumbo* shrimp."

The two men started cackling like old war buddies. Grinning, I wandered over to Mom, Yvonne Williams, and Sandy, who sat in folding chairs talking to Sandy's best friend, Philly Newton. Philly's eyes grew big when she saw me.

"Wanna fight?" she asked.

Philly is pretty stout and fit. When we were little, she used to beat me in wrestling all the time.

"Maybe later," I said. "I ate too many shrimp."

"Shrimp," she said. "That's lame."

Yvonne Williams laughed. "It really doesn't get any lower than that, Tom," she said.

I grinned. "Hey, where's Dad?"

"I just saw him heading outside," said Mom. "I heard he has a visitor."

"Cool. I'll go check it out," I said.

"Yeah, run, you coward," said Philly. She and Sandy snickered like insane teenage girls as I walked away. Which, of course, is *exactly* what they were.

Outside, in front of the tower, I saw Dad standing in the drop-off circle, leaning into a black limousine. I strolled over and found him talking to Randall Foger. Dad turned and smiled at me.

"Hey, son," he said. "Randall just dropped by to thank us for helping Andy clear his name."

I almost snorted. But then I said, "Well, Andy did most of the work. We just tried to keep his spirits up."

Randall Foger actually chuckled at this. "Look, Tom, I don't have any illusions about my son. But he did take some initiative in contacting you about my predicament. I appreciate that you, uh, well . . . that you didn't just toss him out on his ear."

"Honestly, sir," I said, "we couldn't have done it without him."

Mr. Foger nodded. "Well, be that as it may, I guess I have to congratulate you on winning the Department of Energy bid," he said to Dad. "As

I no longer have an entry in the competition, your Mega-Worm wins by default."

Dad got a look on his face. I knew the look. It's one of my favorite looks, actually.

He said, "You know, Randall . . . your Mole performed *remarkably* well yesterday."

"Oh, did it?" said Mr. Foger.

"Yes," replied Dad. "And this contract will be a big, *big* project. We may need to subcontract a lot of the component work . . . perhaps as much as half the contract. Maybe we could work out some sort of—"

But Mr. Foger cut him off. "No thanks, Tom," he said with a dark smile. "We'd just come to blows eventually."

Dad grinned at that. "Okay. But the offer stands."

"We've got a couple of defense contracts that look good for us," said Mr. Foger. "We'll get back on our feet. Then I can get back to crushing you and your puny company."

"I look forward to it," said Dad.

Mr. Foger nodded to him, then to me. He reached out and pulled the limo door shut with a solid *thunk!*

The long car veered around the drop-off circle and headed out to the road.

Dad just stood there shaking his head.

"Somewhere inside that dark beast is a beating heart," he said.

"I know you guys were business partners," I said. "But were you friends, too?"

Dad nodded. "I think so. Of course, Randall would never admit that."

We strolled back into the lobby. The band was just swinging into a Thelonious Monk tune.

"That's good jazz," he said, his eyes lighting up. "I love that stuff."

We stood together for a few seconds listening to the music. I knew that the moment wouldn't last long. People would soon come up and chat, ask how we were, how it all went down yesterday, and so forth. It was a party, after all.

But just for a moment, I had the urge to throw a big Chameleon Cloak over both of us so we could disappear from the world. Then we could just stand there awhile, listening to our favorite music together.

Maybe I could run a few new ideas past my mentor.

You see, I'd been thinking about adding a nano-coating of sound dampeners to the camouflage fabric . . .

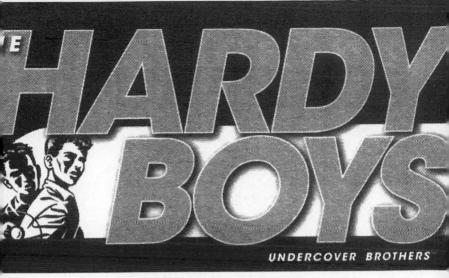

THE HARDY BOYS

BOYS

UNDERCOVER BROTHERS

They've got motorcycles,
their cases are ripped from the headlines,
and they work for ATAC:
American Teens Against Crime.

CRIMINALS, BEWARE:
THE HARDY BOYS ARE
ON YOUR TRAIL!

Frank and Joe are telling all-new stories of crime,
danger, death-defying stunts, mystery, and teamwork.

Ready? Set? Fire it up!

PENDRAGON

Bobby Pendragon is a seemingly normal fourteen-year-old boy.
He has a family, a home, and a possible new girlfriend. But
something happens to Bobby that changes his life forever.

HE IS CHOSEN TO DETERMINE
THE COURSE OF HUMAN EXISTENCE.

Pulled away from the comfort of his family and suburban
home, Bobby is launched into the middle of an immense,
interdimensional conflict involving racial tensions, threatened ecosystems, and more. It's a journey of danger and
discovery for Bobby, and his success or failure will do nothing
less than determine the fate of the world. . . .

PENDRAGON

by D. J. MacHale

Book One: The Merchant of Death
Book Two: The Lost City of Faar
Book Three: The Never War
Book Four: The Reality Bug
Book Five: Black Water

Coming Soon: Book Six: The Rivers of Zadaa

From Aladdin Paperbacks • Published by Simon & Schuster

ALL THE

SPYGEAR

BOOKS WILL SOON BE REVEALED

Spy
them
now

BOOK 1:
The Secret of Stoneship Woods

BOOK 2:
The Massively Multiplayer Mystery

BOOK 3:
The Quantum Quandary

BOOK 4:
The Doomsday Dust

Be
on the
lookout
for

BOOK 5:
The Shrieking Shadow